LAUGH TRACK

LAUGH TRACK

David Galef

UNIVERSITY PRESS OF MISSISSIPPI   JACKSON

The stories in *Laugh Track* are works of fiction. Names, characters, incidents, and places are fictitious or are used fictitiously. The characters are products of the author's imagination and do not represent any actual persons.

Some of the stories in this collection appeared in slightly different versions in the following publications: "You" in *Shenandoah*, "Triptych" and "And Dwelt in a Separate House" in *The South Carolina Review*, "Portrait of a Portrayal" in *Weber Studies*, "Butch" in *North Dakota Quarterly*, "The Jury" in *Writ*, "Laugh Track" in *The Gettysburg Review*, "The Web of Möbius" in *Portland Review*, "The Work of Art in the Age of Mechanical Reproduction" in *The Laurel Review*, "The Inner Child" in *Connecticut Review*, "Metafiction" in *Clackamas Literary Review*, and "The Landlord" in *The Prague Revue*.

I'm grateful to my friends, family, colleagues, former teachers, students, and previous editors for their encouragement, help, and advice.

www.upress.state.ms.us

Library of Congress Cataloging-in-Publication Data

Galef, David.
    Laugh track / David Galef.
        p. cm.
    ISBN 1-57806-422-8 (alk. paper)
    1. United States—Social life and customs—20th century—Fiction. 2. Americans—Foreign countries—Fiction. I. Title.

PS3557.A41148 L3 2002
813'.54—dc21   2001026903

British Library Cataloging-in-Publication Data available

for my father

CONTENTS

vii

I

YOU

IT'S A WARM DAY in July, swelling toward the heat of noon, and your mother is hanging the wash out to dry. The sheets go on the line stretched between the maple and the fence, while the clothing gets draped over the lattice-shaped hanger in the backyard. The scene is familiar enough, your mother humming a Rodgers & Hart song, "Blue Room," as she hangs and pins, but she moves with a grace unknown to you. She is wearing a white sleeveless blouse, her bare arms flashing in the sun. Her blue-checked skirt looks new and swings left and right as she moves. The array of damp wash is slowly spread out like a carefully worked-out pattern, colored shirts and white socks against the darker hues of trousers. The proportion of clothes to clothespins happens to work out perfectly, a neat serendipitous touch.

Your mother steps back to survey her handiwork, looking around her as if there were laundry thieves about. She really just likes to make sure of her surroundings, you remember that. She stands in a rectangle of green, a white picket fence skirting the prim lawn. The sign sagging on the bough of the maple reads #929. Along Pierce Avenue runs a double row of elm trees, shading the pavement like green umbrellas. Cobblestones poke through the pavement where the tar has worn through. A plane

3

drones lazily through a patch of sky. The sound hangs in the air long after the plane has disappeared into the sun.

The job is done, and your mother picks up the basket and walks back into the house. She and your father live on the second floor, the bottom floor being occupied by a family named Bisquet. The kitchen has a four-burner range and a refrigerator that doesn't keep ice well on a hot day like this. The bedroom is cooler, the blue shades drawn, casting blue darkness. The double bed is in the exact center of the room, flanked by twin night tables: a jar of cold cream and a paperback novel facedown on the right one, an ashtray and some loose change on the left. Hanging above the dresser is a 1958 calendar, with the words "FEDERAL INSURANCE" and a pastel of lilacs above the month.

The time in the kitchen reads 10:30, the second hand gliding over the face of the clock like a golden needle. A breeze arises from nowhere, and through the open window comes the scent of midsummer leaves mingled with the smell of hot tar. A neutral wave of heat follows. Your mother opens the refrigerator, extracts what ice is salvageable, and uses it to stir up some lemonade. She sits there at the kitchen table, savoring the tart sweetness, lifting the glass to press against her forehead. The house is strangely quiet, as if it lacked some familiar presence.

At noon, she goes out to shop, carrying a string bag for groceries. She is shorter than you remember her, probably because she is walking in tennis shoes, though she holds herself youthfully erect. By now, the heat of the day has slowed things down to a crawl: people stand under awnings, away from the glare of the sidewalks, waiting for cars to pass in a soft shudder of wind. At the store, there is casual talk about the weather and upcoming vacations (no one is going anywhere, but everyone knows someone who is). The frozen food section, with its change of climate, attracts a lot of customers.

What to buy, what to make? Rib roast is 69 cents a pound, but a heavy dinner like that would be unbearable on a day like this. She picks up a package of rice, some salad greens, a can of consommé—jellied consommé will go down just right on a night like this—and maybe some cold ham. She also has some items written down on a list, but the list has gotten lost somewhere, so she improvises. Spaghetti, lemons, toothpaste. At the checkout, the bill comes to $3.69, not cheap but affordable.

A few years ago, your father and mother were living in a cramped apartment in the Chicago Loop while he attended medical school there, and the room was so small that the bed had to be shifted every time the door was opened, but things are different now. They moved to this address in the Bronx two years ago, when your father began his psychiatric residency at Einstein Hospital, a short commute in a blue Plymouth they have just bought. Prosperity, jokes your father, who was born in 1929, is just around the corner.

On the way home from Williamsbridge Road, your mother buys a packet of loose-leaf paper for a notebook: she is taking education courses at the Bank Street School in Manhattan two days a week, and she has already filled sixty pages with seamlessly cursive writing. When she gets back, the consommé and ham go in the refrigerator, the rice goes into the airless cupboard, and she goes into the bedroom to change into another blouse. She glances at the paperback novel on the night table, O'Hara's *Butterfield 8*, but decides in favor of virtue: the education text for her course *Problems in Teaching the Disadvantaged Student*. The book, a hardcover monstrosity, is for some reason in the bathroom, on top of a copy of *Bazaar*. Outside, she appropriates the backyard hammock—it is really the Bisquets'—and lies down to study.

It is impossible, or nearly so, to take notes in a hammock. The ropes creak and sway, the fabric curls around her in a tipsy embrace and threatens to dump her every time she makes any sudden moves with her pencil. Finally, she gives up and lies very still, looking up at the sky where a whale-shaped cloud is passing with the slowness of a barge. In the bushes, the cicadas are vibrating at the frequency of the heat, plus or is it minus forty?—something your father told her. Something she will one day tell you, but you never will get the formula straight.

A car passes on the street; the scuffing of shoes on the sidewalk approaches, and a neighbor's doorbell rings: a two-tone chime, carried aloft by the lightest of breezes. The humpbacked cloud is now directly overhead, obscuring the sun, the cicadas wailing as if in sudden alarm. But the figure in the hammock lies still, with one hand trailing down, invisibly connected to the book lying on the grass. Your mother has fallen asleep.

Though she has a plain face, a snub nose and a mouth a bit too wide for the contours of her face, there is a certain serenity to her features, a calmness which in sleep is heightened to a thing of beauty. Her eyes are delicately shut, her throat an arch of white bared to the sun. Her flanks are held firmly in place by the hug of the hammock; her breast rises and falls in a slow curve. It is three o'clock.

And what about your father? At about this time, he is in an ivory-white room, interviewing a patient who exhibits symptoms of schizophrenic withdrawal. The patient, a man named Halloran, has been admitted to Ward B, which designates psychiatric problems of a medium severity. At the moment, Halloran is staring down at the twisted knots of his fingers, having made his last comment two minutes ago. Your father waits, placing his own hands face-down on the desk. The soft burr of a table fan blows through the office, an unprepossessing interior with a few padded chairs, a rack of books, and the desk. This year, your father is one of the chief residents, meaning that he supervises other residents on their cases. Short-term work is what he does most of, since the rule of patient-stay at Einstein is a few months at most, followed by discharge or transfer to state facilities. The work is challenging enough, but as a third-year resident he is thinking more and more of starting his own practice.

From the corridor comes the sound of a door slamming, which seems to wake Halloran. He looks across the desk as if calculating the distance between himself and the doctor. He mutters that he feels damn low, and your father nods, referring to a sheet in front of him. Halloran has been out of work since he divorced his wife, and before hospitalization spent most of his time on the street outside his apartment. Removing him to the relative calm of the ward has helped, but he shows no real sign of improvement.

Your father sighs. After this session he will wander down to the residents' lounge and pour himself some iced coffee from the thermos your mother packed for him this morning. In winter, hot coffee with a little sugar mixed in; in summer, iced coffee with milk. The question is, how does the thermos know to keep one cold and the other hot? This is a standing joke between your mother and father, eventually shortened to *How does it know?* and one of a growing number of tag lines that will fly about you during your childhood.

At four, your father meets with a second-year resident named Kaufman to discuss the progress of a woman convinced she is pregnant, though all tests show negative. The other residents seem to like your father: he is matter-of-fact but sympathetic, and he works hard to gain the trust of people. In his tie and shirt-sleeves, he presents a professional front nonetheless amenable to social pursuits—on several occasions, the Kaufmans have been invited over for drinks.

The fan whirs on, the glare of the day subsiding to a bright rust on the blinds by five o'clock. As a rule, your father keeps the room a shade darker than outside to relax his patients, but more than once he has gone to the window to see what he is missing. In between patients, he looks out from the fourth floor of the nursing residence: his landscape includes a hot-dog vendor on a stretch of sidewalk, and the Pelham Parkway half-hidden behind greenery.

At five-thirty he signs out, driving home in the Plymouth with a pride of ownership that borders on true joy. It is the first non-used car he has ever owned, without any wondering where those cigarette burns in the upholstery came from, or who made those nicks in the dashboard. Any marks of experience on this car will be his and his alone—or his wife's. He has promised to teach her how to drive, maybe in August when he has two weeks off. He thinks of her at home, starting the laundry as he left for work, and speculates as to what she is doing now. The day is already cooling down, the Bronx air blowing through the open car window, and he thinks maybe he will surprise her. They can go out to dinner, maybe to that new Italian restaurant that just opened on White Plains Road.

Your mother has just started boiling the water for the rice when she hears the car pull up by the curb. The car door slams with its own peculiar *shoonk*, and in a minute he comes into the kitchen, his tie loosened, his jacket over his shoulder, his brown hair appealingly swept back from the car ride.

The scene is more formal and at the same time more affectionate than it will be in later years. He carefully drapes his jacket over the kitchen stool; she puts down the can opener. He opens his arms wide enough for a battleship to come cruising in, and she flows toward him. A long hug and a kiss, or LH & K, as your father calls it, a panacea for life's blues. He says the boiling water smells heavenly, but it needs a touch of something. She says just wait for the canned ham, which she bought with her own two hands. Actually, her sense of humor is much better than her cooking, and

it was your father who taught her how to prepare her first omelette, on a defective hotplate in Chicago. He nibbles on her ear,
murmuring something about hors d'oeuvres—you used to think
he was actually eating her ear and would scream for him to stop.

I know you're already boiling—the water, I mean—but how
about eating out? That new Italian place.

She takes almost half a second before saying yes. The boiling
water gets dumped in the sink, and the two of them go out to the
car. It's a short drive to the restaurant, almost too short to warrant
the use of a car, but 1) your father likes maneuvering in the new
car, and 2) he has promised to go over the functions of the car bit
by bit. Tonight he demonstrates the clutch as she takes mental
notes (she will turn out to be a far better driver than he, a suprem-
acy he never learns to accept).

The restaurant is called Adolfo's, the lettering in red icing script
on the neat Neapolitan awning. They are seated by a red-aproned
waiter with slicked-back hair and given red plastic menus with an
improbably long list of items. She chooses lasagna and he decides
on the spaghetti marinara, with an antipasto first. She picks out
the black olives and the artichoke hearts while he gets the salami
and anchovies. The entrees arrive suspiciously soon, both swimming in a sea of red sauce. This may be the first of what your
father will call, as he inserts his fork, the parting of the Red Sea.
Still, at the time they are both pleased and decide they will come
back some night, maybe with the Kaufmans. Spumoni for dessert,
and mock-espresso—your mother grew up in New York City and
knows the real thing from the times her father would take her to
Little Italy, but says nothing.

As usual, she is able to locate at least one intriguing fellow
diner, in this case a balding gentleman with a balloon of a head
and three stiffly waxed mustaches, tucking into a platter of clams.
Your mother has the habit of people-watching, and an amazing

facility for starting conversations with people. Before your father pays the check, she has found out that the man is a bus driver on the B6 route, though he also sings semi-professionally. He even gives lessons, but she regretfully refuses: she is studying to be a teacher. Of what kind? For disturbed children. Difficult, he murmurs into his napkin. And your husband? A doctor. He nods over this wise choice. You will have a fine family, he predicts. When they leave, he stops eating to wave goodbye.

The sun has already gone down, but there are still threads of light around the trees when they get out of the car at home. Your father gallantly opens the screen door for her as she fumbles for her keys, as she will fumble before every keyhole in her life. Once inside, she generously shares the last of her refrigerated lemonade with your father. He makes an exaggerated pucker—he likes it with more sugar—and enters the bedroom.

All the laundry lies neatly on the bed: your mother had time to bring it in and fold it, but then she had to start dinner. Slowly, your father starts putting away shirts, socks, pants, and skirts. He halts before a brassiere and is fingering it absently as your mother walks in. He turns. Will the owner of a white Maidenform bra, size . . . 36 C, please report to the bed?

He can be flippant about anything. It makes him charming; it makes him infuriating. Just now your mother succumbs to his charm, sliding onto the bed with practiced ease, her skirt hiking up to show the sweep of her thighs. The night is warm, inviting. He reaches out to stroke her leg, and she draws his hand upwards. Shifting so that he lies alongside her, he unbuttons the top of her blouse. Her arm goes around the back of his neck, feeling the bristles on his nape where he had his hair cut last week. He bends over to kiss her, her tongue invading his mouth, the warmth of her like the day's heat in the shape of a woman.

A shirt, a blouse, a skirt, and a pair of pants land on top of the laundry piles, which get shoved aside. The blue curtains part for a night breeze, street air that plays over their bodies, making the skin delightful to the touch. Your father traces beautiful patterns on your mother's back. She reaches around to tickle his inner thighs, then his groin. In the course of their play, a bra identical to the one on the laundry pile goes sailing onto the floor. A pair of men's Jockey briefs, waist 32, flies in the opposite direction, followed by a pair of white bloomers. She still wears that type, after all these years.

The bed creaks pleasantly under their combined weight, as she yields with his movements, the two of them intertwined, with the cracked beige ceiling above them and the Bisquet family below them, the laundry about their feet, and after it's over he rolls off her stomach and says what next?

Nine months later, you are born in Jacoby Hospital. March 27, 1959, at three in the afternoon. As for all the rest, it can be figured out later.

TRIPTYCH

THERE IS SOMETHING remarkably sophisticated about an eight-year-old who spells *sitting* as *cyddinge*. Annoying, too, thought Dorothy, who was correcting spelling tests for her third-grade class during her lunch break. She had just come across Donald Feinberg's paper—of course, it would be Donald. Whereas other students had left out the second *t*, a mistake reassuringly familiar, Donald's performance had a willful air. It was the kind of improvisation made by someone who knows quite well how to spell a word and has gotten bored with it. The rest of his exam, she noted quickly, was perfect. She looked at the anomalous *cyddinge* again. It almost looked as if Donald had lately been reading Welsh.

At the beginning of the semester, she might have written, "Can you fix this?" and gone right on to the next paper. By now, however, she was beginning to regard everything Donald did as a challenge. She licked the end of her pen thoughtfully; after a moment, she wrote, "Who are you kyddinge?" in the margin. If there had been any sympathetic souls in the faculty room, she would have shown the test to them and maybe asked for advice. But the other teachers at Forest Ridge seemed either callous or singularly unhelpful. Mr. Clay, who taught the third-grade class across the hall, mused on her complaints with an "Interesting, interesting," as if to imply that she created strange problems of her own. Ms. Altern, the assistant principal, kindly ignored her questions—what to do when one of her students brought in a pornographic magazine, for instance. It was her first semester of real teaching, and she had expected a bit more support from the better experienced contingent. In general, she thought she was doing well, but would have welcomed a second opinion to that effect.

She sighed, a sound echoed by the janitor cleaning up around the dining area. He was a bent-over old man with the name *Jerry* embroidered over his left pocket. She wondered if he could spell *sitting*. When he looked up in her direction, she tried a tentative smile, but she didn't like the grin she got in return and went back to grading. Penmanship, she mentally noted as her pen skimmed down a paper that looked like a seismograph tracing. She wrote several model letters beside the last word, *geography*: an *e* and an *a* and a *g*, which all looked alike in the student's version. "Try to be neater," she wrote in painstakingly exact script across the top of the student's paper, and moved on. She finished the papers concomitant with the last bite of her sandwich, then bundled her spelling tests into her briefcase and her paper bag into the trash.

Outside, a ragged line of children were pursuing a playground ball over the asphalt, and she recognized a few of her charges: Robby Sanders, large for his age and truculent; Debra Hauser, always picked up after school in a black limousine. Donald wasn't among the group. Having skipped second grade, he was a year younger than the rest of the class and didn't get along well with any of them. Oddly, they didn't even bully him; they just steered clear of him. Lately, Dorothy had been thinking a lot about Donald, worrying whether he was developing into a problem student, but also just curious about how he functioned. With his pale white face and horn-rimmed glasses, he seemed like an outsider in the world of arithmetic and scholastic readers, a visiting scholar, perhaps, disdainful of rote and preferring his own idiosyncratic approach. The second day of multiplication tables, for example, he had brought in a slide rule. His reading level was impossible to determine. One day, she had seen a collection of Ambrose Bierce sticking out from his desk. On the other hand, he seemed to stumble over the simple stories they read in class, though it might just have been boredom. And any questions were met with the same unfocused stare, which she had decided was one part hostile and two parts bemused. Something would have to be done, but what and how remained unresolved.

As she got up to leave, she saw Mr. Clay trudge in, nodding vaguely to one and all. She had observed his class once, finding it fairly dull, with the students in back circulating among themselves a private communication of their own. And what was her class like from the back? she occasionally wondered. On a whim, she returned to her classroom early and stood at the rear of the room: she surveyed the round table in the reading area; the Nature Corner, with its leaf tracings; the blackboard, clean but with the familiar stippled look of use. If I were a third-grader, she decided, I'd be very pleased to be in Dorothy Weller's class. She sat down at one of the desks and was still absorbed in the view when a few of the children came back in for the afternoon. Someone tapped her on the shoulder.

It was Donald, looking official. "Ms. Weller?" he said.

"Yes, Donald, what is it?" A request for a protractor, a signed permission slip to study physics instead of taking gym?

Donald extended his soft pink hand, laying it on the desk. His brown eyes stared through the thick plastic lenses. "Excuse me, but you're sitting in my seat."

*

Dorothy got home around four, dropping her bag on the kitchen table. In the tiny living room of her apartment, really an adjunct to the hall, the red light on the answering machine flashed on and off. It turned out to be a message from David, witty and character- istically short: "Working late—oh, what a fate—will call back at eight." Dorothy listened to it twice, trying to figure out whether it was rehearsed; then she erased the tape. David worked for the advertising firm of Allen & Shaw, and many of his quips had the sound of copywriting. It was a phenomenon she had noticed when she first met him, at a party given by a mutual friend. When she had remarked that he sounded like an advertisement, he retaliated by calling her a talking blackboard. Their ensuing relationship was based on an odd combination of badinage and endearment that at times was quite intimate, though lately David had been somewhat distant. She did try to be understanding but wasn't sure she was being understood. She debated now whether to phone him at the office, but decided against it. Waiting for his call at eight would give her something to work toward.

She got up to put away her groceries, bought at the Shopwell on the way home. In an absentminded mood, she almost put her teacher's notebook in the refrigerator, but its blue cover made an odd contrast against the embryonic green lettuce, and she re- trieved the notebook with a mutter about getting senile. It cheered her to mutter to herself, to mumble insults for her ears alone: it was something she emphatically could not do in the classroom. Another thing she couldn't do on the job was to take a nap, and though she'd never felt the urge before she began the job at Forest Ridge, teaching a host of third-graders made for a peak exhaustion level sometime around two in the afternoon. In order to get any preparation done for the next day, she found it necessary when she got home to lie down and shut her eyes for a bit, even if she didn't actually sleep. The brief hiatus put a distance between that day's class and the next; it cleared her mind. Otherwise, she found herself muddled: the notebook in the refrigerator, for example, or treating David as one of her students.

She wandered toward the bedroom, stopping before the dresser to let down her hair, which she usually put up in a neat bun for class. She could already visualize herself lying down, resting her head on the pillow. It was almost six by the time she woke up, the room shadowy with the reddish dusk of October. Her head felt fuzzy—a cup of tea would help—and she padded into the kitchen to fulfill the sequence of events she had envisioned before. As the kettle built up steam, she took out her lesson-plan book and laid it alongside a third-level reader entitled *Where Does the Sun Sleep at Night?* These days, the class was doing group reading three times a week, working on the first half of the multiplication tables, and writing occasional stories on family themes. Next week, she would start on a history program for grades five and under, which the principal, Mr. Fannon, was pushing with bureaucratic enthusiasm. After she had absorbed half a cup of tea, she took out her pen and began making notes in her book, planning out spelling tests, book reports, and follow-directions assignments. As David had said one night, watching her, she was creating the pattern for a little world.

By seven, she had put the finishing touches on Wednesday's pattern, with some of Thursday and Friday sketched out. She shut her book, stowed the materials in her bag, and put the bag by the door, where she would pick it up on her way out the next morning. It was a trick she had learned from her father, who, unlike her, never let the office work in his briefcase get any farther into the house than the table by the door. Jobs, he had said, are divided into those you bring home with you and those you don't. It was clear which type he favored, but then he was a man who could rigidly compartmentalize his life. For her, one activity tended to merge with another, and ideas for new class projects came to her while she was packing her lunch in the morning: take a brown paper bag and fold it into halves, then fourths, then eighths (can you do thirds?). David, on the other hand, seemed to be all job these days—maybe the world was divided into three types, or twenty, or as many types as there were individuals. Start counting backwards from five billion by threes and don't stop until—

Dinner. Turning on the radio for company, she managed to banish all thoughts of school as she chopped up peppers, onions, and mushrooms and stirred them into a bowl with two eggs and some Cheddar cheese. She ate her omelette with a bit of salad and a hunk of bread, as the radio serenaded her with an old Bing Crosby rendition of "I'll Be Seeing You." The kitchen walls seemed to draw comfortingly near, and she finished her meal with another cup of tea and a lemon cookie. She fiddled with the crossword puzzle from the *Globe* and had just filled in a three-letter word for "flightless bird" when the phone rang.

She had forgotten to disconnect the answering machine but picked up on the second ring, cutting off her own voice telling callers she was unable to come to the phone. "Never mind that, I'm here," she told the receiver.

"Screening your calls?" asked David slyly. "Who were you expecting?"

"As a matter of fact, you. I just forgot to turn off the machine— it's been a hard day." She told him about her Nature Corner, with all the different kinds of leaves pasted on red construction paper. Students did tracings of the basic oak, maple, and sycamore shapes; they were also supposed to bring in their own samples. Donald, she recalled, had brought in a yellowish six-pointer that no one, not even Ms. Grafton the amateur naturalist who taught art, had been able to identify. Asked where he had found it, he had said, "Around."

David listened dutifully, then launched into his own perora-

tion, which had to do with a client who wanted seventeen treat-
ments of a campaign for a new deodorant soap. She interjected a
few questions about the sales slogans, also asking about his boss,
a domineering man named Dubrowski whom she knew David disliked. At the end of the question-and-answer period, she wondered
wistfully whether he might be coming over, but he didn't think
so, at least not tonight, he was too tired. They left it at that, with
a promise for Friday night and maybe going to a movie.

"I want us to see more of each other again—I miss you." Those
were the words that should have come out, but they remained
unused at the end of the call. She hung up, irritated at herself for
not speaking up more.

"Maybe I should take elocution lessons," she told her answering machine, but the console, having been turned off, said nothing.
A snapshot of David, propped inside the nearby bookshelf, also
forbore to comment. He smiled down from his place on the shelf,
a lanky figure in a sports jacket, with a handsome head just half a
size too small for the rest of his body. It suddenly occurred to her
that there should be a picture of both of them—something else to
ask about, one of these days.

The rest of the evening passed in a brief walk and a few chapters
of an Ayn Rand novel. She went to bed early, woke up in the middle of the night, and couldn't drift off again until she had heated
up some warm milk for herself. She went to school the next morning with a new theme in mind for an assignment: "Seven Things
to Do When You Can't Sleep." Donald came up with ten, one involving palindromes. He signed his paper Dlanod Grebnief.

*

Over the course of the next few weeks, class proceeded fairly normally, or as normally as it ever did. One of the girls had a fight
with a second-grade boy during recess, hurting his right arm and

his dignity. Someone stole the SRA reading cards, which were later found in an empty desk. Dorothy started giving stars for those who had passed their multiplication tables up to 8 × 8, which made some students quite pleased and others dejected ("But you've got to find some way of motivating them," said Mr. Clay, in one of his *ex cathedra* moments). For the time being, Donald was cooperative, contributing to the class discussion when he was called on, and filling in maps along with the other students during geography—though he kept questioning Dorothy as to why any country should be any particular color. "Just color them in," she was on the point of snapping, but instead murmured something about how it was all a matter of choice. Donald turned away, and later handed in a map of Africa that featured stripes and plaids.

"Inventive—maybe we can hire him away from you," commented David when she told him. He was in a good mood that night, having just finished an assignment on a new brand of mayonnaise. He appeared at her apartment by seven, straight from the office, with a presentation jar of mayonnaise in tissue paper. She was happy again—this was the type of inspired lunacy that had originally attracted her to him—and they spent the evening thinking up new uses for the product, about half of which were obscene and two of which they tried in bed. Sex with David was often more fun than genuinely stimulating: at his best, he had a risible quality that transferred itself, his putty fingers tickling her rib cage, his kisses deliberately slurpy. He called her Dotty. Patiently, she waited for the relationship to move into the next phase, but by mid-November it took a step backward again.

He would plead the pressures of work, but it seemed more than that, as if a certain period of affection guaranteed an equal and opposite reaction later. If she asked him what he was thinking, he would snap, "Nothing." Sometimes, even being in bed together made her feel all the more alone. She would wake up in the middle of the night and see him hunched on his side, as if he were moving away from her even in his sleep. He began leaving early in the morning, carrying his shoes out of the bedroom so as not to wake her—she watched him through half-shut eyes. She would have preferred a ruder intimacy, more David. Not sharing, she would have called it in class. There were other details: in the cold weather, without telling her, he had begun growing a beard. With his unobtrusive features, it soon took over too much of his face, but the one time she mentioned the word *foliage* he became first embarrassed, then annoyed. She had dreams of herself as Delilah, creeping up on him with a scissors while he slept.

Near the end of November, she had to fill out progress reports for the twenty-three students in her class. They should have been fairly automatic: by now, she knew who excelled at writing but had a fear of math, who didn't work well with his peers or had an attitude problem. The problem was translating all that she knew into a series of boxes to be checked off: excellent, very good, unsatisfactory. And the space at the bottom for a comment was really too brief for all she had to say. Donald, for instance, came across inadequately as "Bright, but has a motivational problem." For several days, the kitchen table was covered over with report forms in various stages of completion ("Just get it *done*," said Mr. Clay, who handed his in early). But she wanted to be busy, since it took her mind off other matters.

When the first snow came, she held a cutout snowflake contest in class, the students voting on which they liked most, with the three best pasted to a triple panel of oaktag at the back of the classroom. The trouble began there, with Donald protesting that two of the three designs were asymmetrical. The angles were off, or something—Dorothy dutifully listened to Donald's complaint, uncomfortably aware that he was giving the class another reason to dislike him. But he was eminently practical, and he wasn't arguing out of envy. As she knew, the snowflake in the middle of the display, an intricate geometric pattern that grew feathery at the edges, was marked on the back by the initials DF.

So it was the principle of the thing—with Donald, it was always one principle or another—and finally, just to silence him for a while, she told him loftily that it was a question of art. The other two snowflakes weren't flawed but simply depended on a different perspective. He thought a moment, glasses aslant, his small lips pursed. It seemed from his attitude not as if he couldn't answer but whether it was worth revealing what he knew. Finally, he said nothing, and walked out to join the other children at recess. Dorothy watched him go with a certain misgiving. In the days that followed, he began doing more of what she called withholding, talking only when spoken to twice, and committing what Dorothy was sure were deliberate misspellings: *alryte, reddie*. She preserved a delicate silence but felt genuinely cheated: what Donald was doing wasn't fair, not to himself or to her. He got a C on a math test for being off by factors of a hundred: he'd simply added double zeros everywhere. "Interesting," commented Mr. Clay when she told him about Donald's recent performance, though he added, "He's just spiting himself to spite you, don't you see. You might want to have a talk with his parents—that sometimes helps."

Dorothy nodded. It was a possibility she had considered, but lately she had been distracted and thought she would put off the decision until January. One of the distractions, of course, was David: he had become harder to reach, and his answering machine now featured an advertising jingle followed by a voice that offered "Your message in this space, for a limited time only."

"David, this is Dorothy. *Call me*," she would tell the machine, and sometimes he did and sometimes he didn't. Seasonal rush at the agency, he told her when she complained, and she reserved judgment. But they met less frequently, and in restaurants more than either's apartment. On the now-rare occasions when they slept together, he would stroke her abstractedly, making her feel like a piece of sculpture.

The last school days in December were hellish. The kids tracked mud and slush in and out of the classroom, they wouldn't concentrate on the activities she assigned them, and it was all she could do to be tolerant. One Thursday, after a particularly soulless night with David, she stood in front of the blackboard and saw a band of pink-faced savages, sticky-fingered and stupid, dragging her down in a sea of bubble gum, broken pencils, galoshes, and snow pants. The one student who offered a higher level of intelligence was still withholding—Donald, from the back of the room, frowned curiously at her but said nothing.

*

Unaccountably, David had reformed again by the holidays. She spent Christmas Eve and Christmas Day with him, and he was much more demonstrative than usual, buying her an expensive brand of perfume ("*not* a client of ours"). He looked eagerly for the smile on her face when she opened up the package. She had bought him a book of aphorisms, which he solemnly pledged to read from cover to cover. They holed up in his apartment for the two days, taking the phone off the hook, leaving only for meals and a movie. They were, Dorothy felt for the first time, a couple, and they did things a couple would do: window-shopping together, holding each other, and just talking without any particular need to amuse or get across information. They also spent a good amount of the day in bed, and there was a point when Dorothy, her thigh lying lazily against David's flank, felt privy to a small piece of eternity. As it turned out, David wasn't able to spend New Year's with her—his grandmother chose an inconvenient time to enter a hospital in Florida—but Dorothy began the new year with renewed hopes of a more permanent arrangement. She knew now just why she had put up with David's intransigence for so long: David was charming.

*

Back in the classroom on January 3, she found that nothing had magically changed: the students had returned with all their mannerisms intact, including an inability to stop whispering at the back of the room and a tendency to hand in homework late. Students who lagged in reading skills continued to stumble over words; a new triptych of snowflakes went up on the back wall, and class proceeded as before. In certain minor areas, it was possible to see progress: Jenny Larkin mastering the nines in the multiplication chart, or Bobby Randall finally writing a book report that didn't look as if his parents had helped with it.

Others, however, seemed to backslide. One student, for example, who had been a voracious reader, now seemed more interested in model planes. And Donald, for whom it was never clear when he was learning and when he was simply going through the motions, began rebelling altogether. A month ago, Donald's math test might have been partly wrong, but simply because he had crossed out some of the easier examples and inserted his own problems and answers. Now, she would be correcting tests and find that his entire test was a fabrication. Once, when she called on him during round-robin poetry reading in small groups, he began to read a quirky poem which she at first thought was his but later identified as Ogden Nash.

"Donald, why won't you read what's in front of you?"

He made a shove-away gesture, his small shoulders hunching. "Because I read it already."

"Well, then," she prodded, "why don't you read it again?"

"Don't you like Ogden Nash?"

Dorothy did, in fact, like Nash, but thought it unwise to say so. Instead, she gave a practiced sigh and launched into a short lecture about cooperation. Donald nodded, clearly unconvinced, a scholar being told that he had to practice his interpersonal skills. Perhaps he believed that she knew more than he did, but only because she had gone through the texts already. Something had to change, and Dorothy did what she was best at: biding her time.

Over the course of the next week, several incidents occurred. The landlord told her he was raising the rent by thirty dollars a month. In class, Donald performed a nasty color experiment with Magic Markers that turned out to be indelible. And on Saturday night, as Dorothy was eating dinner with David for the first time in two weeks, he told her he was seeing someone else.

They were at a small Indian restaurant they had been to a few times before. The softly draped white tablecloths and flickering candles made for a stagily romantic ambience, and at first she thought he was leading up to something completely different. How endearing that he can't find the right words for once, she smiled. But then the confession came out, and she felt slightly sick. The woman's name was Katherine, and he had been with her off and on for a year. He had spent New Year's at her place in Worcester. He went on, not quite looking at her. His voice sounded weighted down, as if circumstances had settled heavily upon it. "I'm sorry . . . if I haven't called. I've been through a lot these past months."

"So have I."

"Oh? Oh, you mean with me. I guess you have. Look, I didn't intend any of this, you know."

"Maybe you didn't." She wasn't sure what he intended, or what she believed anymore. But he kept on explaining, and eventually she couldn't take it anymore and left the restaurant. That night, she didn't sleep at all. Oddly, the one person she wanted to call was David, but she visualized the answering machine at the other end of the line. Or worse: a voice from a bedroom where two people were sleeping together—she wondered whether he had told Katherine about her. She wondered whether he nuzzled against Katherine's neck—"my form of necking," he had told her early on in the relationship. Which was now at an end. Dorothy shivered and got up, though it was only four in the morning. She made herself some tea and held on to the warm mug without drinking any of it.

Sunday, she mooned around the apartment, a creature in a bathrobe occasionally looking out the window. The winter sunlight, what there was of it, looked cold and metallic. Recently, in an attempt to add life to her living room, she had bought a potted fern as large as a child, and now she watered it lavishly. It formed a green, sympathetic presence, and she almost felt like talking to it. Still, she couldn't quite articulate her feelings: she wasn't crying; she wasn't relieved. Whatever it was hadn't resolved itself by Sunday night, and going to school Monday morning was an exercise in self-discipline.

The classroom hadn't changed—why had she imagined it would? She collected math tests, assigned a story to be read, and was demonstrating a script capital Q on the blackboard when she noticed a shimmering aura that followed her chalk line. She looked up, and the light played in her eyes. It was Donald, fiddling with a prism at the back of the room. He stopped abruptly, but five minutes later he was at it again, making the class laugh with a rainbow that darted about the room. Dorothy decided to say nothing, but she could hear Mr. Clay's voice intoning, "If you don't walk a bit on them, they'll walk all over you." When recess time came, she told Donald she wanted to talk to him.

She waited until the rest of the students had left for the playground, then shut the door firmly. Donald stood by his desk, avoiding her gaze.

"Sit down."

Donald sat down.

"Do you know why you're here?"

"Here on this planet?"

It was a typical Donald response, and she almost smiled. But that would be giving in, and this time she had no intention of letting him off so easily. She shook her head as she circled toward his desk. "You know what I mean, don't you?"

Donald blinked through his thick glasses, knowing everything.

"Of course you do." She placed both hands on his desk, bending down to be more on his level. He shrank back against his chair as she went on. "Now, look: since the beginning of the year, you've been playing tricks, hiding what you know. Leading me on."

He opened his mouth to say something, but nothing came out. He bit his lip, his hands clenching nervously.

Dorothy moved closer. "Leading me on. When I've been led on enough. You don't know what it's like"—he shook his head quickly—"can't imagine how it feels, can you?" She was now inches away from him, her arms encircling his chair so there was no escape. "I'll tell you," she breathed at him.

She described David: the snappy way he talked, the way he danced into a room, the way he would touch her, and where. She was getting carried away but couldn't stop herself. She touched Donald's smooth cheek; she cupped his chin to command his attention as she detailed the late-night phone calls, the growing concern. He didn't draw back but stayed in her grasp, looking stricken as she told him of one flank rising against another, of love in the dark and the separation of days, all the way to the past sleepless nights. "And *now*! Just what does he think—I mean, how am *I* supposed to—?" She shook Donald hard, she kissed him, was clutching him around his frail shoulders for support when she realized what the hell she was doing and where she was.

She took her hands off him, still breathing heavily. She looked around the room—the alphabet, the multiplication tables, her life messily stacked against the third-grade readers—and waited for whatever might happen next.

PORTRAIT OF A
PORTRAYAL

"GRANDPA," remarked Grandma as she stacked the dishes, "was a hard nut to smash."

"Not sure that 'smash' is the right," began my father, looking away—at the carpet, at the sailboat picture on the far wall, anywhere but at his mother. He could never finish his sentences and did not do so now.

"*Imi wakaranai*," muttered Andrea, my thirteen-year-old sister, who had restricted herself to Japanese since early February. No one took much notice, figuring it was just a phase, like her earlier adherence to Finnish. It was just after dinner, all of us ranged around the cracked Formica table in the kitchen, as we each pursued our separate gastronomic processes. My brother, Eric, idly picked his teeth with a tine of his fork; Father belched laboriously. Mother hadn't yet gotten home from teaching, and we were all subconsciously straining to hear the crossing of the threshold as the front door opened and slammed shut. Grandma had lost the thread of her discourse, as she so often did. There was at that moment a comparative rarity in our household: silence.

It didn't last long. Eric removed the fork from its leverage point at a bicuspid and laid it carefully slantwise on the table. "I have supped my full," he announced. "I am no longer esurient." He eyed each of us for a reaction.

"I should think you wouldn't be surly any more, not after three slices of my meatloaf," remarked Grandma, returning to the table with a two-story cake that seemed to have a basement, as well. Her baked goods, whatever else they were, were definitely her own. When the cake was passed to Andrea, she helped herself with chopsticks and proceeded to get a substantial amount in at the right orifice. Father toyed with his portion, gutting the basement and digging a red moat in the surrounding plum jelly. He was really just waiting for Mother to get home, as if she added some finishing touch.

He was right, in a way: Mother did complete things, though mostly other people's sentences. I suppose she came by the habit honestly; she was, after all, an English teacher in the local junior high, in a town that could best be described as ungrammatical. The Baylor household was a haven of correctitude from the savagery outside, or so Mother believed, and instructed us accordingly. Grandma's malapropisms she could do nothing about—how can a woman ever correct her mother-in-law?—but from the first offspring who puled out "Mama," all of us came under what Eric termed, in one of his happier locutions, "the fascist phrase-monger."

The front door creaked open with the familiar sound that Father had been meaning to fix since 1962, ten years ago. There was a longer pause than usual between the creak and the slam, which meant that Mother had packages. Father looked up from the ruins of his cake. His gaze wandered, then settled on me. "Harry, help your mother with." In the foyer, Mother handed me a shopping bag full of Drano bottles (she was addicted to special sales), and I dutifully brought it into the kitchen, where I found a place for it under the sink, next to the twelve cans of Dutch Cleanser and enough steel wool to line a hair shirt.

As the rest of us lingered politely at the table, Mother went into the kitchen and peeled back the aluminum foil surrounding the remnants of the meatloaf. She helped herself to corn and cabbage and one of Grandma's curious rolls: a Parker House with three buttocks instead of two. She sat down opposite Father and began to eat efficiently and without fuss. The smudged makeup and a trace of chalk dust on one shoulder made her look like the victim of an explosion, but she didn't seem to notice. She never noticed her appearance; she noticed others' appearances. In between mouthfuls, she told Eric that he had cake crumbs around his mouth and me that I needed a haircut. Andrea she left alone, probably because Andrea was halfway up the stairs already. Before the threshold of her room, Andrea announced, "*Tadaima*," and took off her shoes. She wouldn't let other people in unless they followed suit.

In another moment, Eric excused himself, though not, of course, in those words. "I must absquatulate," he noted, frowning at us all.

"Can't you even find a chair?" asked Grandma.

Father waved a dismissive hand. "Oh, it's not."

"*That* he's talking about." Mother was already finished with her plate. "Sometimes, I think dictionaries should be kept from children until they know better." In fact, the house was lousy with dictionaries, from the giant Webster's Second Edition to pocket-size glossaries of Serbo-Croatian and Flemish. We had rhyming dictionaries and slang lexicons, Roget's and Fowler's and Partridge's cheek by jowl. We had the Oxford Companion to everything and both the Britannica and the World Book encyclopedia. On the other hand, we didn't own a television set, and if we ever needed to watch something, we went to the Batesons' next door.

I scraped my chair backwards preparatory to rising. It was already seven o'clock. Homework was not a problem in the Baylor household—we all got good grades—but I needed to do some research for an English paper assigned a week ago. "I have to go work," I suggested.

"On that paper you mentioned?" Mother paused, her fork lifted for emphasis. "What did you say you were working on—Conrad, wasn't it?"

I hadn't said what I was working on, and the Conrad reference was purely maternal interpolation. It was up to me whether I followed her educated guesses; it usually depended on what mood I was in. That night, after a better-than-usual supper, I was feeling tractable. "Right, the Conrad paper on, on . . ." I let myself grope, knowing who had hold of the rope at the other end.

"On *Heart of Darkness*, of course," responded Mother brightly. "It's such an enchanting work. It's what I wrote about once for a college essay. Now, what was my point about it?"

I exchanged a look with my father, who shrugged, but then charitably put in a word. Four words, to be precise. "Grace, maybe he doesn't."

"Know where to look? Of course, that's what the library is for. Oh, and Harry, when you're there, would you pick up a book for me? There's a Dorothy Sayers novel waiting for me at the reserve desk. Thanks."

That night at the library, I found more than enough material on Conrad. The adults in Greenvale, if they went there at all, were after the bestsellers, and the kids used the place as a social center. So the real books were always sitting on the shelves, waiting to be taken out for an airing. I decided to check out a biography of Conrad and two books of criticism. I was on my way out when I remembered I hadn't yet read *Heart of Darkness*—Mother always got me muddled this way—so I went back and found that, too. Then I got distracted by a copy of *The New Yorker* (our subscription had lapsed), which I sat down with and paged through for a while. I did the usual, which was to read the spare short story they had and fill in all the gaps.

The divorced character named Sam—I gave him a history that included an education at Yale and an inexplicable stint as a garbage collector. Marjorie, I decided, couldn't connect with Sam because she was really aphasic, which in fact was how her dialogue sounded. The small child in the foreground—it wasn't clear whether it was Sam's or Marjorie's—was actually a dwarf, a guilty reminder of a failed pituitary experiment. And since the story had no ending, I had them all run over, flattened by a huge semi-trailer. That, I thought, was fitting—they were two-dimensional characters anyway.

Eventually, I opened up *Heart of Darkness* and read the first ten pages of that (it would never have gotten published in *The New Yorker*), and by the time I thought of heading home, it was near closing time. I never considered myself an intellectual—Mother said a sixteen-year-old could be at most intellectually inclined—but I did like the library. For one thing, I actually enjoyed looking up facts—and not all of them were in our mammoth home-reference center. So I came to know the public library fairly well, including the two reference librarians, Miss Dodge and Mrs. Cartwright. They were the kind of duo you find in a lot of cheap fiction: Miss Dodge was thin and intent, a steely-eyed, hawk-beaked spinster, guarding those stubby pencils as if they were gold ingots. Mrs. Cartwright, on the other hand, was a jovial, plump woman who handed out bits of information like party favors: a neat citation from *The Beekeeper's Gazette*, for instance, printed on a scrap of paper as small as your finger. Or where to find a description of the mating habits of the kingfisher. Both women knew their reference works; they both knew the whole Baylor family, too. As I headed towards the exit, Mrs. Cartwright called out, "Tell Andrea we have a new Japanese dictionary!"

I turned back to thank her, and a girl named Ellen Crowley from my World Civ. class caught my eye. She was there with her friends, cracking jokes and cracking gum. When I smiled weakly at her, she returned the smile—but I knew I was being smiled at, not to. Walking home through decaying sidewalk snow, I whipped my grungy snorkel coat tighter around myself (Mother had bought three of them on sale, five years earlier). Suddenly, I had a vision of my family all sitting around the table, wearing space helmets. And kids like Ellen Crowley pointing and gaping, having grasped us as the aliens we were.

When I was around Andrea's age, I didn't mind so much. I could always go back to my book on the couch, and I always did. It was a way of ignoring any and all frustrations, particularly ones connected to family. At wit's end over Grandma's garblings (which I could detect by the age of five)? Go read a James Thurber story. Tired of Father's maundering incompletion? Take up Nabokov, linguist extraordinaire—I read *Lolita* when I was Lolita's age. I admired the vocabulary, but I had to take the lust on faith.

Of course, the real problem was Mother. She didn't just run your life, she ran your sentences. I knew she meant well, but that only made it worse, since then I felt guilty about my annoyance and had to compensate in some pretty bizarre ways. You really had to experience her for a while to know what I mean. And it wasn't just me. I'm fairly sure she drove my sister to become a polyglot and my brother to the far reaches of sesquipedalianism. As for myself, I was actually mute for a good seven months, but I eventually recovered. Or at least stopped being mute.

When I took stock of myself the month before (I did it twice a year in a double column of "assets" and "problems"), I decided I was moving toward normalcy. Or maybe the other kids were moving in my direction. Some had started wearing glasses, the end of playground games had shaken out a discernible intelligentsia, and there were even a few I could talk to. People whose conversation wasn't restricted to rock-music lyrics—which Mother parsed in derision—and baseball statistics—my father's one move in that direction was to take Eric and me to a doubleheader at Shea four years earlier, when all three of us had been overtaken by boredom.

Only at this point I was facing a new problem, something I felt I should have gotten to a long time ago. Maybe it was hormonal, or maybe different families just emphasized it earlier. Or maybe it even had to do with baseball—developing your body or something. It wasn't a subject much mentioned in the Baylor household, though it wasn't that any of us was a prude.

The subject was sex.

On paper, I was an expert. I read the Kinsey report when I was in the fifth grade, and any orifices left out I learned from Terry Southern's *Candy*. In fact, I take it back—it wasn't sex, exactly. I just had this urge—I don't know quite how to explain it; when I try, I lose my articulacy—if I saw a girl nearby, I wanted to *do* something for her. Write a sonnet, stand on my head, slay a dragon—anything to please her. And this was true even if I didn't know who the girl was—*particularly* if I didn't know who she was. Because it may have been gonadal urgings, but one thing cooled my ardor like ice in the bed: when she opened her mouth and out came gobbledegook.

She nattered on about the latest Bronson movie she'd seen, and I couldn't help wondering if she knew how to spell. If she told me she liked going to the beach, I got an image of radio-cassette players, sand, and sunlight so strong I couldn't read. She said her brother had a green MG, and I thought about how Grandma once innocently described herself: "I haven't a car in the world." I couldn't help it: I heard a grammar mistake, and it was as if she had corn stuck between her teeth. I suspect my mother had something to do with this. I kept meaning to read Freud, but I hadn't got to him yet.

I thought about all this as I was walking back (alone) from the library. Halfway home, I remembered that I'd forgotten to pick up the Sayers book for Mother. When I got in, Grandma was sitting in what we euphemistically called our parlor but which was really an extension of the hall. She was darning socks the way only grandmothers can, so that the toe or heel grows a thickened patch of mismatched wool. She looked up and remarked that it must be colder than eyes outside. Who nose? I told her, and she bobbed her knitting in affirmation.

I went upstairs to work on my history homework, which this week meant reading about Jacksonian democracy. Jackson, it seemed, was a boob and a half, but that just made him all the more popular. You can see it in the classroom; you can see it in politics: America distrusts brains. Which made for disgruntlement in the Baylor household. As for politics: my father hadn't taken an interest in elections since the last time Adlai Stevenson ran.

Around nine o'clock, Grandma went into the kitchen to make some cocoa, and the drifting scent of hot chocolate eventually brought the rest of us in. Even Andrea, who must have been struggling through her Spanish homework in Japanese. She had already gotten two letters from the dean, but Mother had recently intervened, clearing the way for Andrea to get credit for her waywardness. The six of us shared four mugs of cocoa and three marshmallows in our communal but restless way.

Eric stirred what was temporarily his cocoa. "Deliquescent," he said.

Grandma looked surprised. "At this hour? Eric, they'll all be closed."

"*Dajare*," responded Andrea, mugless but with a brown mustache from her last sip of my father's.

I don't know what it was—family-induced claustrophobia, the abrupt memory of Ellen Crowley grinning at me—but I banged down my mug on the Formica. I had no plan, not even any idea where my resolution was coming from. But I was going to get myself a girl. My family looked at me in surprise. They so often read my thoughts that it was funny, then, how they couldn't see what was on my mind.

My father simply raised his eyebrows—halfway.

"I take it you've finished," said Mother quietly, reaching with a sponge to absorb the pool around the mug.

I nodded, getting up from the table. "One man with courage makes a majority," I told them (Jackson) as I went upstairs to plan strategy. Eric and Andrea weren't the only ones who could be obfuscatory—and I had at least two years on them.

Unfortunately, everything that seemed inevitable the night before seemed awfully hypothetical in the cold gray light of the classroom. How could you attract a member of the opposite sex? Kingfishers did it by waving their brilliant plumage, with a special mating call. I was wearing a brown sweater Grandma had damned—make that darned—and had no idea what constituted a good opening line. "Haven't I met you somewhere before?" wouldn't do—of course I'd met her before; I met these girls every day—I just didn't know any of them. "Haven't I known you somewhere before?" was what a character said in a fantasy novel I read once, but he was talking about reincarnation.

And whom would I ask? There was Trudy Simmons in my trigonometry class: she understood circles and lines, and in the world of angles she struck me as acute rather than obtuse. She had no curves to speak of—but then, I didn't intend to bisect her triangle, did I? Peggy Traub in my history section had a figure so well developed she looked like a sofa, the one I used to fit in perfectly in our living room and where I read books in one sitting (or lying), before

I grew too tall and started reading longer books. Anyway, Peggy already seemed to be attached, frequently at the hip and shoulder, to a large, unfriendly football player named Mike or Ike. Cathy Dunbar was bookish, or at least she carried around a lot of books. But she dressed impeccably, everything color coordinated, making a rag-patch creature like me a bit suspicious.

Try a variety. Don't throw all your eggs into one bucket, Grandma would say. But I didn't know any of these girls well enough, I realized. Harry, you don't know anyone well enough, sniped the small, shrill voice that also reminded me of minor courtesies and dental appointments. It was true: all things considered, I'd rather have taken out a book.

This was what I was trying to change. Can a person will himself to mature?

Nothing ventured, nothing, as my father would have mumbled. The hall bell clanged, and it was time for English class. In the honors section, we were discussing Hemingway, an author I had always hated and would dearly have loved to point out why, but that day my tongue was busy exploring my teeth, particularly the two front ones with a slight gap between them. I made what Eric would have called a susurrus. The closest I got to an approach was bumping into statuesque Jane Smithson as I was leaving class. "Excuse me," I muttered, and she acknowledged my excuse with a nod.

It was no use. I just couldn't—what's the phrase?—make contact. My head was stuffed with plots of novels and arcane words. Not one person in my family was good at socializing. So why did I still want a girl? Why did the Man in the Iron Mask ever want to leave his cozy cell? Didn't he have enough to read in the Bastille?

The rest of the day passed, as they say, in a fog—something like those miniature rainclouds that loom over the heads of cartoon characters. I'm not even sure what I was thinking at any point, though I do remember getting on the lunch line twice; that, and staring intently at a pigeon outside the window of the chemistry lab, wondering whether flying was worth having hollow bones and eating worms for breakfast. When another pigeon began pecking amorously at the first, I looked away.

I've also forgotten most of the walk home from school that day, but I do recall the last hundred yards because that's when I came up with the solution. A little man above me scattered the fog and installed a lightbulb over my head. All of a sudden, the winter surroundings looked bluer, greener. I ran into the house, fended off Grandma's offer of a little gnash, went to my room, and shut the door. For over a month, I had been teaching myself to type on the assumption that it was a Useful Skill. I slipped a sheet of virgin (but corrasable) paper around the roller of the family's Olympia portable. Only then I couldn't think where to start. I looked out my window, with an overhead view of the backyard birdfeeder taken over by the squirrels. A bluejay chattered angrily nearby. Past the picket fence, our neighbor's son Bobby Bateson was playing catch with a friend of his, using a grimy snowball scooped up from the worn coat on the lawn. Plop, smack, plop, as the snowball grew ever smaller. I turned away and looked hard at the wall in front of me, which was basic beige with no pattern at all. I began to type.

When I came down for dinner that night, I had an announcement to make. The family was grouped around the table, investigating a greenish soup that Grandma had just brought out.

"*Taberarenai*," murmured Andrea, poling the depths with a chopstick.

My father took a tentative sip and nodded at the rest of us. "It's spinach. Spinach is good for."

"Iron and vitamins," prompted Mother. She spooned a mouthful. "This is really quite tasty."

"I have a green thumb," Grandma allowed.

Eric's silence was eloquent.

With all this competition, it was difficult to intrude a comment from left field, in a conversation already way out of the ballpark. So I sipped my soup, bided my time, sawed through some leathery liver, and over dessert mentioned that I had met a girl named Isabel at school.

"Oh?" Mother's casual gaze was a pose, I knew.

It was Grandma who got to the point and asked what about Isabel.

I didn't know where to start exactly. I had pages and pages on her, but no specific beginning. I knew her preference in beverages: lemon tea, the same color as her hair. She wore oversized oval glasses, and she could read Proust in the original but was too polite to mention it. She lived on the top floor of a row house with her mother, who worked as a reference librarian; her father never sent the alimony check on time; her favorite place was up in the attic; she had a habit of biting her nails; the color of her underwear was—but as you can see, I had no idea where to begin.

"How did you," asked you-know-who. Instead of waiting for Mother, I answered.

"I met her after school. She, uh, dropped her books." This wasn't in the script, but I suddenly realized that, if I gave away certain details I'd written, people might begin to investigate. In fact, I mentally deleted her last name; she would just be Isabel. Despite this studied vagueness, I was able to pique the curiosity of everyone around the table. Even Andrea asked a puzzled *"Dare?"* ("Who?")

During the next week, I added dimension to Isabel, including the tactile sense. Her hands were warm and delicate, but clammy as Cape Cod when she got nervous. Her yellow hair was hopelessly split, soft as breath. I elaborated; I extrapolated; here and there I interpolated, for my benefit as well as that of others. She wrote poetry, though she knew it was no good. She'd always wanted a dog, but space was a problem, so she kept a pet mouse named Roland instead. And she cared for me. I was happy then, I think, but all stories have to come to an end.

What happened to Isabel after that? We talked a lot, and even went out on dates several times. Once we saw a French movie that both of us wittily dissected afterwards. Another time, she dragged me dancing. I almost met her mother, but I drew the line there, literally. My family was getting too nosy. Also, one or two of her traits bothered me: the affected way she held her teacup, for example, and her vehement dislike of P. G. Wodehouse. I thought of trying to reform her, but I couldn't face the job of revision. Eventually, we broke up, which is to say that I fell in love with a new character, an older, dark-haired woman named Dolores. She had a soft, almost pained maternal look, and knew things that Isabel did not. But she had a husband, and soon I got lost in the extramarital complications.

So I created another woman and a whole supporting cast, including an intelligent male friend for myself, though the sense of competition finally got on my nerves. I began again. And again and again, because I found I liked it and I was clearly improving. Which is to say that I became a writer. And I lost some of my uncertainty, though I've retained my self-consciousness. My early stories are littered with pieces of my dreams, like shards of glass on a threadbare rug. They're quite visible, but you have to be careful in picking them out. My later stories are far more embroidered—you might get lost in the weave.

I do worry occasionally about the success of my creations, about their relative welfare after I send them forth. I also leave occasional threads hanging. You may have certain questions yourself. Did I ever find a woman? Have I matured in other ways? And what of my family, my dear, demented family—how have they taken to all of this? Do you, in the end, believe in them at all? If I showed you how I made them all up, would it bother you?

BUTCH

THE SUN slanted down at an angle of four o'clock. The city had been baking for hours, and by this time of day a low, languorous heat emanated from the sidewalks. Taxis rode with their windows up in air-conditioned silence, and doormen stood under the shadows of awnings. On the rooftop of a Fifth Avenue apartment in the upper Eighties, an elderly man named Butch Delaney sat stiffly in an orange deck chair. He was stripped to the waist and glaring off at a point on the horizon, the sun glaring back from the Hudson. His attitude suggested that he had come up to the roof not to tan his body but to show that he could take it.

Half an hour longer in the heat, and Butch decided it was enough. He got up, inhaled heavily, and began collapsing the chair. When he stood up, his chest sagged with age, and his arms were afflicted with a light palsy. Still, at one time he had been quite broad around the shoulders, and he maintained an oddly wasp-waisted appearance, his plaid bathing trunks hanging on to the last remnant of his former physique.

The chair took too long to fold, and he cursed at it, not in any one-word dismissal but in a muttered series of threats. He kicked at the chair, threatening to mangle its aluminum frame or cut off one of its legs. "Runty chair, you with a bad case of rickets, you rat, if you want to see another sunset, you'd better fold up." He spoke with a gangster's drawl but even slower, at the speed of a man in his seventies. He was half-joking, but then there was the other half. Once, Butch had been with Ed Hoffer's gang dealing liquor and dope during Prohibition. He had broken men's arms and was not to be stopped by an uncooperative piece of furniture. A grunt, a sudden exertion, and the chair collapsed. Butch bent down, shouldered it, and walked inside. He took the elevator down to the eighth floor, whistling "Meet Me in St. Louis." Butch was a man of parts.

He fiddled with the keys at the door of 8C and walked in. The only other person in the apartment was the black cleaning lady, who came in on Mondays and Thursdays. Her name was Mabel and she was just putting the sheets on the double bed in the master bedroom after finishing with the smaller room down the hall. It was a cavernous apartment, with a kitchen, a scullery, two bedrooms, and a giant living room merging into a dining room under a chandelier. Butch had acquired the place from a late friend of his in the early 1950s when he thought it was time to settle down. His wife, Maureen, had been twenty years his junior but had been fragile, like the chandelier in the dining room. She had tinkled and shone bright for guests and had died in her thirtieth year.

The Delaneys had one daughter, Samantha, who grew up in the small bedroom, going to private schools on the upper East Side and occasionally emerging from her room, all dressed up in lace, to be presented by Butch to his evening guests. Often there would be parties, elegant men in tuxedos and women in dangerously low evening gowns, and Samantha would watch the drinking and occasional fighting from her bedroom door. She was Daddy's little girl because Butch always told her so, but she dropped out of Bennington when she was nineteen and since then kept afloat on a tide of boyfriends. Occasionally, she came back home in tears, letting herself in late at night and sleeping in her old bedroom. By

Butch's orders, Mabel was to leave everything in Samantha's room absolutely alone.

Mabel came out from Butch's room with a sheet folded over her arm. She wore a black-on-white uniform and a permanent pout. "I'm almost finished with the beds, Mistah Delaney. You wan' me fix you somethin' for your dinner 'fore I go?" She stared painfully hard, as if it broke her heart to address him.

"What?" Butch had been thinking of Samantha, who was supposed to drop by tonight with a friend. That phrase "with a friend." He leaned the chair against the wall. "What did you say?"

"I *said*, would you like me to fix you something to eat before I leave? Some chicken, maybe, or some sand'ches?"

"No. No, don't bother. Samantha's coming over tonight, and I'll order something from Jimmy's." Jimmy's was a rather fashionable Italian restaurant off Madison Avenue where Butch knew the owner. He fixed Mabel with a dismissive gaze. "Just finish with the beds and go."

"All right." Mabel looked disapproving but tramped back to the bedroom. Butch wanted to take a nap—the sun had hollowed him out—but he had to wait for Mabel to finish.

In the meantime, he put away the chair in a closet and walked into the kitchen. There wasn't much in the cupboards or the refrigerator except for crackers and coffee, frozen vegetables, and a few jars and cans. There were lunch fixings for Mabel and whatever else she said was needed. But mostly it was a kitchen of relics. Butch usually went out or had food brought in. He had never learned to prepare food, and Maureen had been too rare a creature to cook. The garlicky Italian dishes Butch liked were best enjoyed in a restaurant anyway. His doctor had recently cautioned him against too much oil and spices, so Butch had gone to another doctor. His heart was living faster than the rest of his body, or something.

He poured himself a glass of iced tea and wandered back into the living room to drink it. He sank into a deep wing chair. A gilt-framed picture of Maureen rested on a stand between two marble ashtrays, Maureen in a strapless evening gown on New Year's Eve, 1959. She knew what she was marrying but was hopeful of reforming him. They had met halfway somewhere, with him wearing slippers around the apartment and her acquiring a taste for gin. She was never much of a mother but had stayed elegant to the end. Another picture in a silver oval frame, Samantha graduating from high school, looked down from the third shelf of a break-front. Somewhat like her mother now. There was a light spot on the wall where a youthful picture of Butch had hung for years: snap-brim hat, double-breasted suit, and a suitably shady background, but Butch had taken it down when Samantha left. The whole apartment had been the same for years out of Butch's misplaced sense of inertia. Now it was 1975, and he had nothing to compare himself to except the memory of the day before.

There was a full-length mirror in the hallway, and he was struck with the sudden urge to look himself over. He got up with a lurch—sitting out in the sun had made him woozy, or light-headed, or something. A green spot floated between him and the mirror.

As it faded away, he saw himself in the darkness of the hallway. He reached back to flick on the hall light. He snapped into clarity, the corners of his mouth tightening. In front of him was a tall, elderly man, slightly stooped, clad in bathing suit and sandals. He still had his straw pale hair, though it was wispy, and his blue eyes looked washed out. He had once stared a man named Gutsy Fagan into the ground with those eyes. Maureen had said they were his best feature but could never hold his gaze. He concentrated, trying to intimidate the man in the mirror, but he blinked and then his eyes began to water. Hell. He looked away.

His own interior lighting was going bad, too many shadows. Living alone did it. Sometimes at night, seated in the wing chair, he would lean back into the dim interior of a speakeasy, maybe Delaney's that used to be on 49th Street, with its round wobbly tables and a few dim shapes in back listening to "Ain't She Sweet?" And there he was, sitting at the table nearest the band with two other gentlemen. None of them had taken off his hat; all smoked stogies, screening themselves in a protective blue cloud. Butch was obviously protection for the other two: he had those shoulders that made tailored suits a necessity, and even sitting down he bulked above the other two. They were the McHallan twins, or they looked like the McHallans, and they kept staring nervously toward the entrance. Twice, the black velvet curtain in place of a door parted, but once it was a woman in a silver lamé gown and the second time it was a tuxedo who didn't matter. Neither of the McHallans touched his drink; Butch blew a perfect smoke ring at the woman in the silver lamé gown.

The music from the band shifted suddenly to a dirty rope of jazz, twisting just out of range. Suddenly, one of the McHallans knocked over his drink. The brown liquid spilled onto the table, flowing into a puddle which grew larger and larger, flooding everything in clear brown as if the scene behind it were varnished. Everything froze like an old daguerreotype, then the image simply faded into nothingness.

"You want anything before I leave?"

Butch blinked, no longer in the picture. Mabel had changed to street clothes and was eyeing him narrowly. He gave her a look. "Repeat that."

"I *said*, I'm leaving now. Anything else before I go?"

"No. No, go ahead." He groped for his shirtsleeves, but of course he wasn't wearing a shirt, he had been sunbathing. Sleepy. He needed a nap. His sandals slapped against the floor as he walked into the bedroom and pulled down the blinds. The front door shut with a slam, and that was Mabel. He pulled down the bedcovers, the sheets still smelling of fresh bleach. The McHallan brothers hadn't died that night; they were shot months later, by which time Butch was working for a bootlegger named Corry Sullivan. Once he had resolved that point, his mind felt clearer. He lay back with his head against the pillow and promised himself no dreams.

He awoke to a darkened room, the clock on the night table faintly luminescent. He had never suffered that momentary confusion that others feel upon waking; he saw that it was 6:15 and got out of bed at once. For dizziness, take one, two, three deep breaths. He picked out a gray suit and pencil-stripe shirt and started to dress. Samantha was supposed to come at 6:30, and though she was usually late, he would damn well be ready on time. His hands shook a bit when he selected his tie—his touch of palsy—but he could still tie a Windsor knot without benefit of a mirror. There had been a time when looking sharp was his business. He wondered about the friend Samantha said she was bringing, probably another of the artist-bums she hung around with. Sincere gravy stains on the jeans, or was it paint, that had been the last one. One day he would find out whether Samantha was acting this way on purpose, or maybe it was just that she was his daughter. Butch adjusted his tie with a precise yank and walked into the living room.

First, fill the ice bucket. Then call Jimmy's and order dinner for three, all the dishes that he liked, which he knew would be all right for Samantha, who at least shared his taste in food. If the man she was with didn't eat Italian food, he could be polite about it and eat it anyway. Butch recalled a meal he had forced himself through, it must have been over forty years ago, with three big Greeks who kept passing him a plate of something that looked like snails and tasted like soap. Everyone with a gat on his person, everyone grinning just like friends.

He grinned now as he emptied a tray of ice cubes into a polished oak bucket. This would be an occasion, no matter how it turned out. Nights alone he had never gotten used to, and though he had taught himself to read books, real books, and even enjoy some of them, he preferred company. Preferably female, and the women had better be smart enough not to treat him like an adorable grandpa. He had paid for a lot of women over the years, after Maureen's death and before, too. They showed more skin these days, more brazen looks, impatient with the formalities. But without the old moves, the game skittered off into nonsense. Not that he practiced pursuit much these days, but flirting still pleased him, and he enjoyed the company of pretty women. If Samantha hadn't turned out gorgeous like Maureen, he wouldn't have known what to do. And she could be attractive and calculating at the same time, a combination Butch was forced to respect.

He checked his watch, 6:30 already, and reached for the phone. He dialed and sat back in the wing chair. Five rings: Jimmy's was busy tonight. The restaurant had outgrown its origins as a red-checkered-tablecloth joint with cheap liquor. The location had been just right for the growing numbers of young professionals in the area, and now the menu was stiff white linen, the prices intimidating. Butch wasn't intimidated; it was never a good idea to be frightened. He had known the proprietor, Louis D'Angelo, a tubby man prone to patterned vests and suspenders, since 1956, the birth of Samantha and the end of Butch's business enterprises.

He waited. On the sixth ring, a castrato voice answered, "Hello, this is Jimmy's."

"This is Butch Delaney." He spoke into the phone with authority, fixing his gaze on a spot above his vanished living room photograph. "Listen, I'd like to order a dinner to be delivered to my apartment."

The voice simpered. "I'm sorry, but Jimmy's doesn't do take-out."

"So? Let me speak to Louis. Even better, let Louis speak to you, and tell him Butch Delaney is on the line."

"I beg your pardon?"

"Butch Delaney. You want me to spell it?"

"No, I don't think that will be necessary. Please hold the line."

Butch held on, grimly, while the voice disappeared for a few minutes and then came back, a little sulky.

"I'm sorry, Mr. Delaney. What would you like to have?"

"That's better. To start with, I'll have the clams casino, three orders, and minestrone. Then veal piccata, two of those, and one shrimp scampi. Don't bother with dessert and coffee. We'll go out for that." This last comment was directed at the photograph of Maureen, who always liked to go to a different café after the main course. Maureen shrugged her bare shoulders adorably. She wanted to go to the Café Versailles for their éclairs, and Samantha, who was only two, had to be left behind with the nurse. She got a lot of sticky good-night kisses and found desserts in paper bags on the breakfast table next morning.

"And when would you like it delivered?"

"Make it seven-thirty. I'll expect it then." And Butch broke the connection. Of course, Louis couldn't be blamed for hiring new people, but the old courtesy disappeared that way. And if the connections weren't there anymore, what good was it living past seventy? He had made a lot of money in the last of his transactions with a Brooklyn building contractor, and this time of life was supposed to be the reward. Sitting in a chair on a Saturday waiting for his daughter to come visit him.

He thought about mixing himself a drink but decided against

it. No need to get back at rudeness with his own rudeness. He could wait. But where the hell was Samantha? He looked at his watch. Close to 7:00, and what would be her excuse this time? She always offered some reason, as if she were trying to make it all logical. The train was late, the heel of her shoe broke, the taxicab had a flat and the cabby had to get out and fix it. And tonight?

There was a key-turning sound at the door. Samantha letting herself in, never getting the three locks open on the first try. There was the sound of a high heel in an impatient tap, the mutter of a male voice. Butch got up from the chair and wrenched open the front door, pulling along the keys in the lock and Samantha's hand with them.

"Good evening." He grinned sourly at Samantha, extracting the keys and giving back her hand. She was wearing a red silk dress and black high heels. She had Maureen's figure, which meant nice calves and bosom, and the same black hair. But she wore too much makeup, possibly because she knew Butch didn't like it. At the gaze of inspection, she pulled back nervously, but she immediately recovered herself. Her lips broadened in a lipsticky smile, and she planted a kiss on his cheek as he bent down to hug her. His Samantha—and someone else, always another man. She gestured backward to accommodate the figure behind her.

"Daddy, this is Albert." She stepped back to allow the two men to shake hands, and Butch got his first good look at the latest acquisition.

"How do you do?"

"Nice to meet ya." Albert was some find. The hand he proffered was like something from an aquarium, damp and fishy, his shirt cuff riding back to reveal several inches of hairy white arm. The cheap cut of his suit made him look slightly askew, his yellow-striped tie held by a big fake-jewel clasp. When he grinned, he showed too many teeth. He had a pencil mustache which looked chewed. Possibly he licked it when he was nervous; he disengaged his hand from Butch's firm grip as soon as he could.

The sleazy appearance didn't bother Butch so much, not compared with the men Samantha usually brought around. Faded jeans, loose white shirts, scraggly beards—he compromised his standards in favor of his daughter. With this one, though, there was an air that Butch couldn't place. It was damned familiar, all the same.

"Well, come in, both of you. Let me build you a drink." He walked to the bar in the far corner of the living room and upended three glasses. "What'll it be?"

"I'd like something cool. How about a gin and tonic?" In point of fact, Samantha always drank gin and tonic, no matter what the climate. She had inherited the taste from her mother, who used to give her a little sip from her own drink.

"Scotch, mine." Albert came over to the bar, watching as Butch measured out more gin than tonic, the way Samantha liked it. And a piece of lime. He filled another glass with ice and poured Johnnie Walker Black Label into it, just past the halfway mark. Then he made a drink for himself, a rye highball, as Albert appraised the bottles on the shelf.

He gave a grudging nod. "Some good stuff here. No cheap alky in stock, heh."

Butch looked sharply at Samantha, who was looking at the portrait of her mother. The reference to cheap alcohol was a low shot at his bootleg days, if that was how it was intended. He wondered how much Samantha had been talking.

"Here's your drink." He handed the scotch to Albert, who took the glass in his left hand and took a healthy gulp. He swallowed, let out some air, and grinned through his yellow teeth. "That hits the spot, don't it."

"Samantha, here's yours." Samantha turned away from her

mother and put her hand on Albert's shoulder. With the other hand, she reached for her drink. Butch watched with narrowed eyes: Samantha usually wasn't so chummy with her pickup acquaintances. Was she just touching Albert or actually leaning on him? Butch's glasses were in the bedroom and he didn't like wearing them for social occasions.

"Here's to cooler days," Samantha suggested, raising her right arm as in a pledge.

"I'll drink to that." Albert favored both of them with another knowing grin and raised his glass, but only part way. There was a tightness under Albert's left armpit, more like a bulge of some kind—and Butch froze with the drink halfway to his lips. Manners, manners, called a professional voice from some inner chamber of his brain, and he took a sip of his rye without tasting it. Don't stare too hard; don't stare at all. Keep the conversation flowing and gradually edge toward the nearest exit.

But that would be inhospitable, even to a man with a gun. From the shape of the bulge—lousy tailoring, lousy concealment—it looked like one of those cheap pieces. Never trust a Saturday night special; it might go off accidentally. In which case Albert would have an ugly hole somewhere in his side. In the meantime, the man was here with Samantha, and Butch owed it to her to be pleasant, though he deplored her taste. At least the artist types came without anything more dangerous than a cigarette lighter.

Albert continued to drink stiff-armed, Samantha oblivious. He finished the drink soon and held the empty glass in front of him.

"Care for another?"

"Sure, why not?"

Butch poured, thinking. In a pinch, he could throw the drink in Albert's face, but then what? Lacking the old speed, he had no follow-up. What should he do, what could he do?—stop pouring scotch, for one. The glass was almost overflowing. Show a little suavity, damn it. He poured off an inch of scotch into the drain at the end of the bar and handed the glass back to Albert. People carry guns for any number of reasons, none of them good. Ignore it?

"I've ordered dinner from Jimmy's, should be here in about fifteen minutes." Samantha nodded, smiling, and he addressed Albert. "I hope you like Italian food."

"Love it." Albert nodded several times for emphasis.

"Good." Butch advanced on Samantha, put his arm around her slim waist, and steered her to a chair. "Why don't we all sit down?"

"Daddy, your whole arm is shaking." Samantha pressed his hand, cool fingers against his. She actually looked concerned, blue eyes wide open.

"Comes with age—I'm all right." Butch disengaged his hand and gestured to another chair. "Siddown—uh, sit down, and we'll drink until dinner."

Albert nodded with a new grin, this one slanted upward left, with just enough room for a coffin-nail cigarette to poke out of the corner of his mouth. He sat down in Butch's wing chair, which made Samantha shift uncomfortably and cross her legs. She knew propriety was being violated. Butch tried to catch her eye, but it was impossible.

"Mind if I smoke?" Albert had a pack of Luckies out, smacking the pack against his palm.

"Go ahead." Now he was staring at Albert. Get the eyes moving again.

"Like one?" A friendly paw offered one to father and daughter, sitting next to each other in two slat-backed chairs. Both declined with thanks, Samantha out of form's sake and Butch because of the one doctor's order he followed. Albert reached into his left jacket pocket and pulled out—Butch stiffened—a flashy metal lighter topped with a jewel. He set fire to his cigarette, sucked in, and puffed out a long stream of smoke. He crossed his legs; his pants leg rode up one white shin.

"Samantha said you used to be in the construction business."

"Yes." What else had she said? There had been no hiding any secrets from Samantha after a certain age. It hadn't seemed necessary. She had listened to him attentively, asked him a few questions—she wanted to know if he had ever killed anybody—and that was that. She wouldn't talk to him. The next year, she had gone off to college and soon dropped out. The first man she had brought home was named Ted and wrote poetry and lasted two months. Samantha had a similar attention span for all her men, who tended to resemble each other. But Albert stood out even when seated.

"I'm in the construction business myself, Brooklyn." Another jet of smoke. "It's a small circle, the construction business in New York. Maybe you knew Pete Heimel?"

Hands shaking again, stop it. Pete Heimel was dead, that was what Butch knew. He even knew who had done it. That was in 1960, after he had officially retired, but he still had contacts. He considered himself lucky to have quit when most of his enemies were out of the picture. Now who was this nobody in front of him, breathing his air? "I heard of him, yeah." No sense in keeping up a blown cover. He squinted at Albert, hard. "Why? Was he a friend of yours?"

"Nah, not him." Another puff: Albert was building himself a smoke screen. "I just figured we had to know some people in common."

Samantha was leaning forward, her elbows on her knees, Butch noticed. It was hard to read her expression, though: absorbed or amused? She caught his gaze and favored him with the most innocent smile imaginable. Albert tapped one mole-brown shoe against the other.

Butch licked his lips nervously. He could make some comment about the weather, about the terrific heat these past few days. He got up from his chair. "It's getting cold in here. I'm going to turn the air-conditioning down." The adjustment panel was in the kitchen.

"Sure." Albert stuck a finger inside his collar and ran it around. Samantha said nothing, watching Albert.

On the way back from the kitchen, Butch heard the downstairs buzzer. Usually it was like a one-minute warning; now it was a welcome sound. "Dinner's here, or it'll be here soon." He willed Samantha to rise, but she stayed seated until Albert got up, slapping down his trouser legs.

In a minute, the waiter from Jimmy's knocked at the door, wheeling a folded-up trolley inside. He had been at Butch's before and knew where to set up. He winked at Butch, who slipped him a ten-spot in advance and called to his guests in the living room. Albert shambled in—that easy walk, as if he owned the place. At a time like this, the proper place for a daughter was by her father's side, Butch felt, and Samantha as if on cue promptly materialized on his left. She really did look attractive tonight in that red dress, and she must have known it. She might have had odd gaps in her education, but she had a thorough knowledge of her assets. She shrugged her smooth shoulders and let Butch pull out her chair. Albert knew well enough not to take Butch's chair at the head of the table and found his own seat across from Samantha.

The waiter was doing a professional job of laying the table: green tablecloth, green cloth napkins, and heavy silverware placed against china. There was a complimentary bottle of wine from Louis, with an apology for the rudeness of one of his employees. Butch nodded thoughtfully upon reading the note. He would have to drop in one night to thank him. Louis was really a good friend, from a vanishing stock.

The three of them sat in silence as the waiter poured the wine, served the soup, and left the other dishes on the table in covered trays.

"I hope you enjoy your meal. Please call the restaurant when you have finished, and we will send someone over to clean up." He bowed as he left the apartment.

Albert waved goodbye with a loose-jointed hand. He reached for his fork and stopped himself. "You people say grace?"

Samantha smiled sympathetically.

"No," said Butch shortly, and began the proceedings by picking up his soup spoon.

For a while, the activity of eating passed for communication among them. Albert ate a lot of the Italian bread with his soup, asking four times for the bread basket. Samantha took delicate sips of her soup until it was half-consumed and then sat with her hands folded in her lap. Inevitably, there was conversation, mostly about the hot spell, a nice safe topic as far as Butch was concerned. He still didn't like the way Samantha agreed with Albert and even seemed to lean across to him during the meal. For once, the veal piccata seemed to be overspiced, or maybe it was the company. His tongue stuck to the roof of his mouth.

They were almost finished with the meal when Albert intruded a different note into the conversation. He finished his veal and pushed away his plate. "That was great food." He grinned at Butch. "Food like that, a swell apartment—you must be pretty well fixed, right?"

Butch put down his fork. A light breeze from nowhere ran against his chest. "I have money, if that's what you mean."

"I think you know what I mean, and you can speak my language, too. I happen to know we're in the same line of business, only now you're retired. How do I know?" Albert rolled his eyes, looking everywhere but across from him. "A little bird told me."

There was a tender feeling growing in Butch's chest, as if the light breeze were blowing through his sternum. Or boring a hole. There was danger here, but it was too late to avoid it. He was in the direct line of fire. Find a confederate. He looked at Samantha, who turned suddenly—and smiled. And kept smiling, the strength of it joined by Albert's grin.

The smile was pitying and said I know you, old man, and you're not what you think you are. If you ever were a big-time gangster, that's all over, it's been over for years, and maybe you can still impress doormen with it. The smile widened and said you've gotten feeble and boring, and I want life, see the man I brought tonight, he has a real gun, he showed it to me. Samantha's eyes flashed in scorn at Butch for just a second, then reasserted their pretty blueness.

His response was pain. The pain was so awful that Butch wondered if Albert hadn't shot him. There was a past to this, but it was consumed in a moment. His chest constricted as if pulled in by fiery threads. He grimaced and put out his hand. That made it worse.

"Are you all right, Daddy?" Neither she nor Albert made any move to get up.

The sudden pain was subsiding now, leveling into a chest-high ache. He remembered once when he had climbed seven flights of stairs with a bullet lodged in his shin—no, that was the man he had shot. He gritted his teeth. "I'm all right. Twinge—of something. I'll be okay in a minute." His own voice sounded funny to him. Could die laughing.

"You should take something for that. I got a friend who works in drugs."

Butch nodded, face set against the pain. If he got up, if he could just straighten himself out . . . he took hold of the armrests and pushed himself upwards, but when he was standing, another pain shot through his chest. A green and yellow pain, sparks under the skin. He groaned and held on to the table.

Samantha looked at him curiously. "I think we should call an ambulance."

"Yeah, good idea. You got the number?"

"I think so." She got up and went to the phone in the kitchen. Butch could hear her voice but not the words. Sound was leaving him in a thin blue trail, like revolver smoke. It wasn't happening; he took a deep breath but exhaled onto the carpet. Or someone did, in excruciatingly slow motion. How had he gotten to the floor? He looked up and saw Albert watching him. Albert was joined by Samantha and they both watched him, the man with the purple face.

"Should we move him to the couch?" Albert cocked an eyebrow at Samantha.

Leave me alone! Butch shouted, but no one heard him.

"No, we might make it worse."

"Hah?"

"Worse than it is." She turned her back on the scene. "I'm going to wait in the living room."

"You're not running out, are you?" He took her hand.

"Of course not." She shook herself free, drew herself up straight, and looked right past the man on the floor. At least it looked that way from Butch's perspective. She spoke: "I'm Butch Delaney's daughter."

Or maybe they said nothing at all.

A bookmaker in Butch's brain started offering odds for survival. Butch took a piece of the 5 to 3 action and roamed the ceiling with his eyes. The voices faded into a gentle buzz, then rose to a hum. Two men in white were walking on top of him, pushing a wheeled ambulance cot. They shimmered as if they were undersea. Reaching down, they levered him onto the cot, and he hardly felt the pain at all, they had surrounded his whole body with gauze. His head lolled to the right, and he got a view of the living room.

Samantha and Albert stood in view like two flat portraits, saying something inaudible. Albert buzzed and Samantha nodded. She moved towards the door.

I want the punk to come along, too, they're both in it, do you hear me? A bubble of spit surfaced and broke on Butch's lips.

Samantha was nodding her head, the first man in white was nodding back, the whole procession moving towards the door. Samantha bent over and brushed her lips against his cheek. His last view as they wheeled him down the hall was of her, waving, retreating, shutting the door behind her. A double cross, he should have known, he of all people should have been prepared. He lay back against the cot, trying to keep his features without expression. Bluff them and he might get out of it yet, there was still a chance. The attendants glided the cot to a halt in front of the elevator and pushed the DOWN button as Butch waited, looking for an out, figuring the odds, biding his time.

THE JURY

By the summer of 1988, I hope for jury duty as a break from my
boring job. The location is right near Chinatown, and the lunch
breaks are said to be long. When a notice arrives in June, I admit
I'm pleased.

*

There is a subtle incentive to be prompt in arriving for jury duty:
the waiting room is divided into comfortable armchairs, straight-
backed chairs, and benches—all filled on a first-come, first-seated
basis.

*

Selecting a jury: as the lawyer's questions are repeated to each potential juror, the phrasing alters, so that one person's answer of
"yes" means the same as another's "no."

*

Jury duty gives you a startling view of just how uneducated a cross
section of the city can be, and how egotistical the rest is.

*

When you get selected for a jury, whatever case it's for, you get an unsinkable feeling, no matter how heavily you wanted to be free of this mess interfering with your work, that you've succeeded in gaining both lawyers' approval, that you've won something valuable. The expressions of the unchosen people in the gallery reinforce this view.

DAY TWO

In his address to the jury, the prosecuting attorney uses metaphor and plot to make his meaning vivid. He talks about his address being like the table of contents to a book, or the edge pieces of a puzzle.

*

Seated at a desk to the left of the judge, a stout, balding, rubicund, yet dour-faced Dickensian character in a business suit fusses with papers and stamps, seals envelopes, and in general creates an atmosphere of quiet activity. Occasionally, he rises and disappears through a small door at the side of the courtroom. He also, in a loud mumble, swears people in.

He turns out to be the court clerk.

*

Note the miracle of the stenotype machine, incredibly rapid yet so silent, the stenographer pausing only every once in a while to ask someone to repeat, or to inspect her fingernails.

*

This case starts with a simple cause, robbery, and begins to blossom: a sawed-off shotgun, a chase, recovery of hidden property, drugs—and an inkling that the victims themselves may have been involved in a drug sale. Sixty-one glassine envelopes of heroin were recovered from one of the robbers.

*

The withdrawn questions and the answers stricken from the record are invariably the most intriguing.

*

The Bible and the truth, so help you God, are still in vogue as a courtroom oath.

*

The acoustics in the courtroom are terrible, muffling some of the evidence.

*

"What do you do for a living?"

"I'm a drug dealer," responds the witness, with an amused shrug.

This same witness keeps referring to the robbers as middle-aged, and it turns out he means twenty-three or twenty-four.

*

The prosecutor establishes a narrative, and the defendant's attorney tries to prove there's no plot. Or, to borrow from the realm of literary criticism: the prosecutor reconstructs and the opposing attorney attempts to deconstruct.

*

How do you judge when both sides are scum?

*

The abyss, the abyss—which abyss? There are so many.

*

Confusion:

1. The man poking the sawed-off shotgun at one of the victims may not have been the man later caught with it in his possession.

2. The policeman heard a shotgun go off, but the two holes in the car were made by a pistol.

3. The BMW was a new 1987 model. No, it was from 1986.

4. The jewelry was the victim's, though it was all borrowed from his friend.

5. The restaurant a bunch of them went to was Spanish or Chinese (probably Cuban).

6. The piece of jewelry in question was a four-fingered ring spelling out "$OZZIE$" in diamonds and gold. It could easily double as a set of brass knuckles.

7. The victim's beeper was for the video shop where he worked for his brother. Or else it was for drug pickups.

A robbery or a drug feud? How do you make one coherent story from these conflicting accounts? One straight point: The witness, later at the restaurant, ordered white rice, beans, and pork chops.

*

Today, at my favorite Chinese coffee shop that I go to during the lunch recess, the flavors seem off, not just one, but all of them, like a shift in a spectrum. Or maybe it's me.

*

Halfway through the second witness's testimony, I get the odd feeling that all this is being staged for our benefit—it is—and that it's all a play—it most definitely is not.

*

When the two lawyers ask to approach the bench, the court stenographer rises to stretch. Both men tend to talk fast, and her hands must be killing her.

*

One reason for a jury of twelve random people: the judge, day after day, gets jaded, whereas we, the jury, are new to this kind of presentation and stay interested in the proceedings.

*

And yet random thoughts occur to you even while listening to expert testimony: the bulge of a woman juror's shorts; what to have for dinner that night.

*

In leaving jury duty on a half-day recess, there is the childish delight of being let out from school early. The difference is that some of us use the newfound time to call in at work and hear what's been going on in our absence.

*

Though I live in a rough area of the city, during my period as a juror I feel that no crimes will be committed against me.

DAY THREE

Life at court:

By the third day, the jurors are acclimated: the announcement of a recess brings out the books in the jurors' bags. It's heartening for a scholarly type like me to see so many people reading, even if it's for lack of any other amusement. In fact, the main waiting room where we were all pre-jurors has a television area with one lone TV. The question, of course, is who gets to decide which channel to watch? Do they decide by forming a committee of twelve?

*

The female-to-male ratio among the members of the jury is two to one. All my women friends have asked me about this.

*

The first witness has a lawyer who sits by him while he is on the stand. He can speak with her before, after, or during the prosecutor's examination—but he doesn't initiate any conversation with her. She does, however, stop the proceedings once to whisper excitedly in his ear.

*

At lunchtime recess, I go to visit my car, parked in a seedy area right near the courthouse. Three bailiffs with pistols hanging from their belts are lounging around it.

*

"While you were in the car, did something unusual happen?"

"I got robbed." This is said with a smile. It's not so unusual in New York.

*

One witness has had so many arrests and convictions that his memory is fogged as to specific charges and dates.

*

There is a boring interval in the proceedings whenever the prosecuting attorney draws out points from a witness that previous witnesses have already stated, even if slightly differently. Corroboration is generally dull; contradiction is interesting.

*

More confusion in the trial:

8. One of the victims stopped dealing drugs a year or two ago, but he's still in the business.

9. One of the robbers actually worked for one of the victims in the car, or bought drugs from him—or never saw him before.

10. Both policemen heard a shotgun blast, and the shotgun, according to a firearms expert, was fired. But the holes in the car were made by something like a .38 pistol. This is the second time this point has been made. Why should repetition help an argument?

*

The firearms expert testifies that the rifle (exhibit C) was fired. What is the difference between a rifle and a shotgun?

*

The third witness appears to be suffering from selective amnesia.

*

Half the jury flinches during a particularly brutal grilling of the witness, while the other half seems to enjoy it.

*

People with a poor vocabulary tend to repeat a lot, though they may make up for it in more vivid body language, even in the witness box. One man jabs the prosecutor with his elbow.

*

Inevitably, someone invokes the Fifth Amendment. Like a dead metaphor revived, it achieves sudden impact in the courtroom.

*

They should strip the witness, strap him into the box, and attach electrodes to him. A red light and a buzzer would go off when he lied, and he would be encouraged by electric shocks.

*

In responding to objections, the judge doesn't use "sustained" or "overruled"; he says "yes" and "no" in a voice as imperturbable as a turgid river. I wonder what he wears under his black robe.

*

The stenography machine has ten double-jointed keys on one level and four on the lower level. The stenographer gives daily recitals like a pianist with mutes on her instrument.

*

Half the lawyers around the building are wearing yellow ties, last season's power color. It gives the jurors something to fixate on.

*

A witness from a municipal records division crosses up the lawyers with conflicting testimony from several official forms. Bureaucracy baffles *everyone*.

*

There's so much extraneous information we have to sift for a conclusion. In other words, the trial is like life.

*

The moment we've all been waiting for: the defendant takes the stand. He turns out to be a drug dealer's bodyguard and says he was only buying drugs from the "victims." During the same deal, he was recovering the jewelry for some cash and some dope.

*

More confusion:

11. The defendant says there was dope and an Uzi submachine gun in the BMW, which contained neither.

12. The jewelry was sold—or borrowed.

*

New characters: Hector, Richie (a.k.a. Don Ramon), and Tony, whose name is so obviously a cover it should really be in quotation marks. Also, Chico, who now happens to be dead.

*

The Uzi was fired once, and then it jammed; this explains the loud report the policemen heard.

*

As the defendant tells his story, the five-foot-tall gilt letters "FRAME-UP" light up over his head.

*

The defendant had two addresses, at 131 Broome Street, Apt. 4E and 22C, and at 210 Rivington. That makes three.

*

There are more drugs, crack and coke, as well as the heroin. But who was the customer and who was the dealer?

*

The defendant's *Weltanschauung*: "I know the stick-up boys, I know the dealers, I know the snitch—I know everyone on the street."

*

Prosecuting attorney: "I see. And you have a personal code of ethics?"
  Defendant: "I don't understand the question."
  Withdrawn.

*

More confusion:
  13. The defendant did or did not know the victims.
  14. The jewelry was at one point exchanged for thirty, fifty, or eighty caps of heroin, worth ten dollars each.

*

Five witnesses have helped to mark up and elaborate the map showing the scene of the alleged crime. The defendant doesn't understand the map.

*

Evidence of assumed lower mental functioning: Prosecutor to defendant—"Now, draw a rectangle. All right, make it a square."

*

Both sides add a few extraneous details to give verisimilitude to their stories—one of which is false. This is not the kind of conflict taught in creative writing classes.

*

The defendant gives twice as much information as the prosecutor wants, which at least is more interesting than being unresponsive, which the prosecutor insists he's being, anyway.

*

The court has told us not to concern ourselves with the second man, Don Ramon, apprehended at the scene, who hasn't been seen or heard from during the trial, so we're not concerned, but we sure as hell are curious.

*

Can't others attest to the relationship or lack of it between the so-called victims and the defendant? This trial seems to be lacking in certain crucial details.

*

End of proceedings for today. I go home bemused. In the middle of the night, I hear sirens go by and wonder if they will end in a case of trial by jury.

DAY FOUR

These are the facts. The facts are these. There are no facts.

*

What seems plausible so far:

Three men were waiting in a borrowed BMW one night when three strangers came by and robbed them at gunpoint. The moment they were allowed to drive away, they went straight to the police, who came back to the scene of the crime and found the three robbers still hanging around. One was apprehended, another was shot, and the third got away.

Or:

The defendant and his cohorts (partners? colleagues?) were making a drug pickup from a parked BMW when suddenly things got ugly. So the defendant pulled out a weapon and took the drugs at gunpoint—and also some jewelry from the men in the car. They made the dealers drive off and stayed around to laugh. No one expected the cops to come ten minutes later. Drug pushers aren't in the habit of calling for the police.

*

Characters on the jury:

Two fair-haired gentlemen in their mid-fifties, one slightly heavier than the other. Both seem to have nothing better to do than serve on a jury and appear delighted to be here.

One older black woman who knits constantly. She has a thick body and massive arms, and to see her fussing with colored yarn is to understand why people enjoy watching dancing bears.

A young black woman who by virtue of first selection is the forewoman of the jury. She seems bright and observant, or maybe the knowledge that she is the forewoman has infected her with a sense of responsibility.

Another black woman, middle-aged, who came in late one day because she had to attend her son's graduation from elementary school. She is perpetually embarrassed—over her lateness, over a comment she has made, over the chair she is sitting in—over anything.

A dyed-red-hair Yuppette, who works out at the Paris Health Club. She is fairly self-assured, though it's not quite clear about what. She dresses in black Reeboks, wide hip-hugger pants, and soft cotton print shirts. She has a punk hairstyle held together with mousse.

Two well-bred white women, one mousy but with a ready smile, interested in operations management and ballet, the other with a habit of crossing her long, attractive legs, but otherwise no character traits distinguishable yet.

One businessman type, the only one who comes to the trial in a suit and tie. He is reading Gore Vidal's *1876*, and you get the feeling he will still be reading it two years from now. He nevertheless is the most informed among us about court procedure and occasionally, during our later deliberations, will quietly answer procedural questions.

One Asian-American, an airline flight attendant who lives close enough to go home for lunch. He tends to be late, and we have more than once sat for ten minutes in the jury box waiting for him to arrive.

A hefty pale woman who speaks with a trace of the South and calls her office frequently to stay in touch. She is reading a huge Danielle Steele novel. When she sits down, her lap spreads to the proportions of a couch.

A frail, elderly woman with white hair like a nimbus. Possibly because she is one of the alternates, she tends to stay removed from all discussion.

One nondescript younger Hispanic woman with a set expression.

And me.

These make up the twelve members of the jury and the two alternates.

*

The prosecutor is a tall man with silvery hair worn long, including a well-kept beard. He is incisive, yet knows how to tell a good story, or how to destroy one. He has a few assistants who sit in the gallery looking distinctly edgy.

The defendant's attorney has a WASP afro that doesn't do much to conceal his receding hairline. He's the same height as the prosecutor, and when the two of them wear a similar suit color they look like two members on the same team. But the defending attorney is testy and fidgety, and withdraws many of his statements before he finishes his sentences.

*

The judge is a middle-aged Hispanic man in black robes, who speaks with rancid butter in his voice. He has a well-developed sense of sarcasm, and he no longer appears as bored as he did at the beginning of the trial. Occasionally, during a particularly convoluted moment between lawyer and witness, he will break in to explain everything.

DAY FIVE

The jury is actually composed of fifteen people; that is, three alternates instead of the usual two. How could I have missed the third one? She is young, with frosted hair and a debonair way of smoking cigarettes that she must have copied from 1940s movies.

*

The prosecution is not required to prove any motive. How absurd.

*

The judge, lawyers, witnesses—what are these people like at home?

*

The three men in the BMW were Victor Gomez, the drug dealer; Oswald Ferrara ("Ozzie"), a former dealer; and Michael Lopez, a kid who just associates with them. The presumed robbers were the defendant Damien Marta, the shady peddler Don Ramon, and a guy named Chico. The owner of the BMW, we learn, was named Williams.

Names don't help.

*

Unanswered questions:

1. Why did Damien and the others hang around the area, considering that by either side's account a shootout had just occurred?

2. If it was a simple robbery, as the witnesses say, why would Damien have pulled off the job with sixty-one envelopes of heroin in his jacket pocket?

3. Why was Damien negotiating a drug deal in a crowded area under a streetlight?

4. How does the motorcycle helmet (exhibit D) fit into any of this?

*

Altogether, seven witnesses have testified: the three alleged victims, two policemen, a firearms expert, a records keeper, and the defendant. That makes eight.

*

"I believe his story is incredible," says the prosecutor. Neat oxymoron.

*

At what point does the perception of additional possibilities become a disadvantage? When do you have too open a mind?

*

During the summing up, the court clerk brings back some dry cleaning and hangs it on the coat rack in back. I wonder how many robes the judge goes through in a week.

*

The summations form two slants that do not add up to the right angle.

*

The judge instructs us to consider nothing outside the evidence presented, but the evidence we heard and saw was insufficient, and the speculative possibilities are fascinating.

*

"Proof beyond a reasonable doubt" is the quantity the judge tells us we are to seek. Interesting how many of us on the jury repeat the old phrase "beyond the shadow of a doubt," which is not the same at all.

*

Of the eleven counts against the defendant, nine have to do with first- or second-degree robbery or attempted robbery (with or without a weapon, and only "attempted" in the instance where one of the men in the car had nothing worth taking). The remaining two charges have to do with unlawful possession of firearms. There is a formal, overlapping redundancy to all the indictments, so that a charge of guilty on one or two is sufficient to convict.

*

We start our deliberations and soon reach lunchtime. Everyone orders coffee with the meal.

*

Reassessment of the jury:

The two mild-mannered gentlemen stay that way, holding to their opinions without saying much. Both are disturbed by the lies on each side.

The older black woman is convinced of Damien's innocence. She has worked as a nurse in that area and knows what street life is like. Eloquent arguments attempting to prove Damien is guilty cause her to withdraw into truculence.

The young forewoman moderates the discussion with a light hand, unsure herself of what she believes. Before the deliberations are over, she will change her verdict twice.

The middle-aged black woman is as adamant as the older woman about Damien's innocence but can't account for the jewelry being where it was. She talks occasionally to poke holes in the "guilty" argument, however.

The businessman enters the deliberation room confident that the accused is guilty. He talks at great length about how flimsy the defense is, and when that works only partly, points out that all we need determine is that the jewelry was taken, for whatever dumb reason and no matter what else went on. Though his glibness puts me off, he has a point, or several.

The Yuppette, originally unsure, becomes more and more outspoken in urging a guilty verdict the more she hears the well-groomed businessman expound. I can't help thinking about what I am wearing: jeans and a lumberjack shirt.

The Asian-American remains silent, doodling on a pad. He smiles shyly when people ask him his opinion.

The two well-bred women have slowly shifted from not guilty to guilty, also swayed by the businessman. They entertain doubts every which way, however.

The hefty woman says nothing for a long while and then announces that she thinks the defendant is guilty. She happens to be in business, I recall. She seems to have weighed the factors in some sort of cost analysis.

I am trying hard to keep an open mind, but it keeps flicking closed like the eyelid of a lizard. What preserves me from any kind of certainty is the conviction that all parties are lying.

The alternates have all left for the day. We are alone.

*

Of course, only the jewelry stolen from one side of the car was ever recovered. Chico made off with the rest, and Chico was never caught, and now Chico is dead.

*

Partial truths are far trickier than outright lies.

*

Okay. Damien and his friends went to make a drug deal that somehow went wrong. Shooting ensued. The rest is fabrication. But the rest is what the trial is all about.

*

These are some rules of the street, volunteered by the heavyset black woman juror, who has experience: First, don't rob anyone you know, especially people who might know where you live. Second, the way drug runners stick to their job descriptions would make a labor union real happy.

*

All the surrounding motives and confusion of detail dissolve into one annoying point: why was the jewelry stolen when there were drugs to be had?

The reconstruction of incidents: order is imposed on the system from without. That means distortion.

*

It's not a question of "Is the witness lying?" By now, most of us think that the witnesses' stories are partly false, but we don't know which part.

*

When we return to the courtroom to rehear evidence, the judge, the court stenographer, the two lawyers and the defendant, even the people in the gallery, are still there as if they never moved, though it's now night.

*

The jury as a whole is a slightly confused but aware individual, talking to itself.

*

Five hours into the deliberations, and tempers are running short: eyes inflamed from cigarette smoke in a small room; necks cricked at angle of 120° from staring at other jury members.

*

The jury breaks for dinner, courtesy of the state, at Stark's Veranda Restaurant, which must be used to parties of twelve.

*

Punchy jurors: "What kind of fish did you order?"
    "Veal. Allegedly."

*

Near the restrooms in the basement of the restaurant, jurors make phone calls they're not supposed to make. This is what being sequestered means.

*

Back to deliberation. Lack of motive, lack of motive. We're not supposed to be considering motive, so we dwell a lot on its absence.

*

If I were a drug dealer, I wouldn't go to the cops, no matter what. I don't think anyone in the jury room is a drug dealer. We lack the right perspective.

*

Someone in the case—most likely everyone involved—is holding something back.

*

At nine P.M., all vote guilty but two, who stick with their gut feelings that the defendant is telling the truth. A few of us who have switched from not guilty to guilty are still half in love with some outlandish hypotheses.

*

The maneuvers of the guilty and not-guilty voters on the jury begin to resemble an endgame in a chess tournament. Neither side has enough left to mate, but the clock is ticking.

*

It's tired and I'm late. Or maybe I mean the other way around.

*

We may have to stay the night, also at the state's expense. This makes us jumpy—one woman, so help me, is afraid of getting AIDS from the hotel sheets. We argue more vehemently about the case, finally deciding to have Damien's testimony read back to us almost in its entirety. Upon rereading, suddenly the details make a lot more sense. Or at least we've managed to fit them into a coherent configuration.

*

Not guilty. Guilty. Not guilty.

*

The judge suggests we adjourn for the night. We protest that we're near a decision. During the nine hours, the majority has moved from not guilty to guilty, and now an amazing resurgence of faith in Damien's testimony has switched most people back to not guilty. When only one guilty vote is left, the pressure is tremendous. We are at a climax.

*

The better narrative triumphs. The defendant's tale is taken over the witnesses' story. The vote becomes unanimous. There are smiles all around. We signal to the bailiff that we've reached a verdict, that we're ready to declare what is, after all, only an opinion.

*

Denouement:

Damien's mother sobs when the verdict of not guilty is read and kisses a few of the jurors outside the courtroom. She tells us that Damien is getting married, that he'll reform.

I see no reason to believe this proposed sequence of events.

LAUGH TRACK

IN HIS THIRD MONTH of psychoanalysis, Rupert Schnayer brought a laugh track to his Wednesday session. Instead of Dr. Blauberg's attentive silence, giggles and guffaws and irregular whoops of laughter punctuated Rupert's free associations. It buoyed Rupert's confidence, though it was, of course, an obvious resistance to the therapy.

"Why?" was Dr. Blauberg's only comment, asked during the subsequent session when Rupert evinced guilt over the episode.

Rupert squirmed slightly on the couch. "Why?" was a difficult question, though he recognized its legitimacy. "To get a few laughs," he finally murmured. And therein lay the problem.

Rupert Schnayer had entered analysis in late August of his thirtieth year because of a certain loathing that made the sight of a blank page a hideous confrontation. Yet he wasn't trying to complete a novel or even write what he once termed "breathless dross." Rupert was a gag writer, and then he was a blocked gag writer and couldn't write any more gags.

"It isn't that I've lost my sense of humor," he complained to Dr. Blauberg—and to anyone else who would listen. "I reread my old material and think it's funny as hell. I just can't duplicate it." He opened a small notebook and propped it on his chest. He read from his latest selections. "Man falls into a coloring vat and dyes a terrible death. Dies and dyes, see? Man appears briefly at a swank dinner party dressed in tux and tails, with an intravenous tube stuck into his arm. Says, 'I haven't even got time to eat and run.' Or this crack about women who overdo it with makeup: 'O ye of little face. . . .' "

He slapped the notebook shut. "You see what I mean—garbage. I'm not married, so it can't be my marriage, though it might be sexual. When I'm with a woman, I feel performance anxiety, and then I don't perform. I feel kind of useless these days, really." He lay on the couch, his eyes vaguely fixed on the ceiling, which had a long, white, diagonal crack in it. He thought a minute and smiled. "I used to write great gags about people with mental problems."

The analysis took off from that point, more or less uneventful until the day when he brought in the laugh track. The next Wednesday, he placed a whoopee cushion under the doctor's chair. They talked about the whoopee cushion as an infantile device to gain attention, but Rupert's repetition compulsion led to similar gags the week after, and the week after that.

"I'm interested in these incidents." Dr. Blauberg was thoughtfully returning a patch of fake dog vomit to Rupert, who lay in stifled paroxysms on the couch. "Do you think of yourself as hostile?"

Rupert came up for air. He stared at the crack in the ceiling and composed himself. Lately, he had abandoned his dog-eared joke books and taken to carrying around Freud's *Jokes and Their Relation to the Unconscious*. At the moment, he was resting his head on it instead of on the blue pillow wedge that matched the couch.

"I suppose it is hostile. And it probably is regression." He fingered the plastic dog vomit and laid it at the end of the couch. From a distance, the puddle looked like a gray hole, as if a large,

Welcome to Orange North Branch Library

You checked out the following:

1. <u>Laugh track</u>
   Author: Galef, David.
   Barcode: 38117001487394 Due:
   9/24/15 11:59 PM

2. <u>On the wild edge : in search of a natural life</u>
   Author: Petersen, David
   Barcode: 38129000610926 Due:
   9/24/15 11:59 PM

You saved:
$52.00 by using
your Orange
North Branch
Library today!

obnoxious beast had taken a bite out of the upholstery. "My usual gags were a hell of a lot more sophisticated than that."

Dr. Blauberg said nothing, and in the encouraging silence Rupert wandered into a memory of his father. Mr. Howard Schnayer had been a pugnacious cigar smoker, a small man prone to flicking ash all over the household rugs and furniture. He had never credited his son with much brains. A short while before he died, he attended a show for which Rupert had written most of the material. He didn't crack a smile and flicked cigar ash on the people sitting next to him. "There was a skit about a cigar smoker during the show, but he never said anything about it. Repression again, I suppose?"

Rupert smiled a winning smile, but the canny Dr. Blauberg was silent, as usual.

"Well, you tell *me* why I'm here, then. It's costing me a small fortune to keep myself spread out on the couch like this. I mean, I'm not used to this, me telling you gags and paying you to listen. A paid audience hurts my self-esteem. What I have left of it. Can you blame me?"

The paid audience shifted in its seat.

"I know you're out there, I can hear you breathing," Rupert muttered. In another five minutes, the session was over, and Rupert went back outside again to confront the world.

After both doors had closed firmly behind Rupert, Dr. Blauberg sighed, got up, and retrieved the plaque of vomit from the couch. Like a careless child, his patient left his toys scattered all over the room, and they had to be picked up. The whoopee cushion had been rediscovered by an elderly female patient right after Rupert's session. The moment she lay down on the couch, an eruption occurred which, in the total honesty of the psychoanalytic situation, was hard to explain. Dr. Blauberg tried hard to preserve his professional demeanor, but after a minute of frustrated apology, even he felt like snarling, "Don't you have a sense of humor?" Later in the day, he jotted down in his memorandum book, "Must not adopt Mr. Schnayer's mannerisms."

Rupert's analysis progressed even as the patient regressed. With his shock of sandy hair and wide-eyed expression of surprise, Rupert looked at times like a boy who had wandered by mistake into a doctor's office. Dr. Blauberg almost felt like slipping him a lollipop. At other times, Rupert was a gloomy, grudging old man, and then he tended to talk about his father. "So I didn't like the bastard. You think I'd stop writing because of him?"

Raised eyebrows.

"If he were around now, he wouldn't stop me writing jokes, he just wouldn't care—no sense of humor, always telling my mother to forget about me, that I was a disgrace to the family. I tried hard to be a disgrace, I really did. Told my mother I wanted to be a garbageman and almost made her faint. My father just smoked at me, didn't say a word. Probably wanted me to grow up like him, cigar and all."

"Do you think maybe you're atoning for the way you acted toward him?"

"Hah?"

The next day, Rupert brought in Freud's monograph on atonement—which in no way atoned for the exploding cigar he gave to the doctor that session. It was a Corona Corona, the scarce prewar kind. Dr. Blauberg thanked Rupert absently and lit it up after dinner that night. He had smoked through half of it when it literally blew up in his face. To calm himself, he read through Freud's "Analysis: Terminable and Interminable" long into the night, puffing on a less ostentatious cigar which he took out of his mouth to inspect occasionally. Never accept gifts from a patient.

Rupert pointed out that he had never played any practical jokes on his father when he was a boy. "My father wasn't a shrink, he worked for a glass factory, did the accounting. Not a funny job. If anyone had told me I'd be a gag writer, I'd have said he was nuts. Now I'm not much of a gag writer anymore, and I think *I'm* going nuts." He was confessing horizontally, his eyes toward the crack in the ceiling, which was beginning to resemble a map of Asia. "You need new plaster," he added, not quite irrelevantly, and lectured the ceiling, "Not another crack out of you."

Dr. Blauberg regarded the crack as an artifact in the treatment and called in the painters on Friday. Unfortunately, the new plaster merely outlined the crack, helpful to Rupert as a fixation point. Dr. Blauberg did think of moving the couch to another part of the room, or even conducting the session in amniotic darkness, but he was really a traditional therapist, and he kept things as they were. The thought crossed and recrossed his mind that he was being too lax. *Am I amused by him, and what if I am?* There were certain problems with the therapy, not the least of which was the interest he felt called upon to show a failed comedian. It was also necessary to keep the frustration level from climbing too high, and Rupert seemed to have a low tolerance. What better way to be heard than to acquire a captive audience of one? In fact, Rupert did have a certain engaging presence, the doctor admitted to himself—must analyze the countertransference, he noted in his book.

At least there were few of the long, embarrassing silences that characterized another of his patients, an obsessive named Garfield who pressed his nose into the soft green of the couch and refused to communicate. "Thif *iv* my comm'cation," he would mumble into the depths of the cushions. At least Rupert Schnayer talked. And as Rupert talked, Dr. Blauberg found himself slipping slowly into the role of straight man for Rupert's gags, a victim of fake telephone messages and other contrived situations. Dr. Blauberg interpreted these incidents as hostility from transference and did not appreciate the embroidered dunce cap sent to him on his fifty-third birthday.

"Your nervousness about your humor seems to have disappeared—how do you feel about that?" Dr. Blauberg was nervously fingering the dunce cap on his desk, wondering whether the damned thing spurted ink at the touch of a hidden button. Rupert hadn't mentioned the cap at all, and it was conceivable that someone else had sent it—conceivable, but unlikely.

"I don't feel one way or the other about it. Things are still pretty blah. I'm writing blah jokes. 'I come from a mixed family: my mother talks Spanish and my father talks dirty.' " He waved his arms, perilously close to knocking over a ceramic vase perched on a nearby table. Dr. Blauberg was looking the other way, so he extended his arm a little farther and really did knock over the vase.

To Dr. Blauberg, it wasn't so much a plea for attention as a broken vase, though he did point out gently, calmly, that unconscious actions were often rooted in deep emotions—resentment, for instance—against a father figure—such as an analyst—or, by displacement, the analyst's vase. As Freud noted, there are no accidents. Rupert walked home in a fog of guilt, replaying in his mind the scene of Dr. Blauberg down on his knees, picking up the pieces of the destroyed vase and placing them in the dunce cap. He gave a guilty laugh.

Rupert missed the next session, but came back the day after with a replacement vase. For once, Dr. Blauberg was suspicious.

"Does it leak like a dribble glass?"

"Why do you ask?"

"Will it break into pieces when I touch it?"

"What?"

"Is this a trick of some kind?"

Rupert folded his arms. "It's not a joke. It cost me forty bucks. I think you suspect me too much." It was a provocative point—

suspect an arsonist of causing a fire?—and it represented a turning point in the analysis, now a year and a half old. "You don't tell any gags, and I'll promise not to psychoanalyze you," was the way Rupert put it.

At least there were no more practical jokes.

They began to work better together, at any rate. In the delicate analytic balance, Dr. Blauberg was becoming slyer, more attuned to Rupert's subtly deranged humor. Conversely, Rupert felt easier about his disclosures, talking more freely about his life. Class clown, college dropout, medium-successful comedy writer, deliberate loner until he began getting lonely, somehow unable to connect with people—classic narcissism, as Dr. Blauberg recognized. Annoyance at his own flaws, anger at others who pointed them out. Half the confessions were riddled with defensive humor, and as the months passed, Rupert talked more and more about his writing instead of the rest of his life. At one point, he announced triumphantly that whatever had been blocking him had now abated. He was currently working on a monologue about a made-up character named Pomfret, and some of the material surfaced one Thursday session.

Dr. Blauberg let Rupert go on about Pomfret until he ran out of material or just decided to quit, in the middle of a situation between Pomfret and a hooker. " 'So sleep it off!' she says, and Pomfret—" Rupert sat up on the couch, as if he had just woken up. "I don't know what got me onto this. Talking about sleep, I guess. Anyway, I'm working for a new agency now, and I was, ah, thinking of quitting therapy." He paused for a moment. *Da da dum.*

There were any number of responses Dr. Blauberg could have interjected. He decided not to comment on Pomfret. The point he chose to stress was that Rupert still exhibited symptoms, his claim of normalcy possibly a flight into health. Dr. Blauberg asked him to think about his decision and waited for a crisis.

The crisis came within a week. "A man walks into a bar, says, 'You pour me any beer in the house, I can tell you where it came from.' So the bartender takes him up on it, pours him some Heineken on tap, and the guy says, 'Holland.' Someone buys him a Pabst, he says Milwaukee; Utica Club—Syracuse, and so on. Finally, a drunk from the other side of the bar slides him an amber glass, the guy takes a sip, and spits it out on the floor. 'Goddamn, this is piss!' 'Sure it is,' says the drunk, 'but *whose*?' "

Dr. Blauberg fidgeted in his Eames chair.

"Wait, I've got another one, a better one. Guy walks into a bar, looking very depressed—he *is* depressed. Says, 'I've just lost my job working for the agency, what do you say to that?' " Rupert turned to look at his analyst. "Well, what do you say to that? I lost my job. They told me I wasn't funny anymore."

"Do *you* think you're funny?"

Rupert didn't answer. Then, after about a minute of staring at the ceiling, he started laughing and crying. "They were right, I wasn't funny anymore, that beer joke has got to be the oldest one in the book, and I've been writing gags just like it. Here—Christ, no, I'll spare you." Instead, he talked about the way he felt in the mornings when he woke up to a hissing radiator that sounded like a bad audience, and then he had to drag himself out of bed to confront the bathroom mirror. "When I shave, I could swear to God it's a trick mirror—you know, the kind that warps all the straight lines. Face like a moldy cheese, belly starting to sag—beginning to look like my father, I think. Wouldn't be so bad, only there's nothing up here anymore, either!" He hit his head hard with his fist. "Do you know I'm sick of myself?"

"Hmmm."

And Dr. Blauberg waited for the post-catharsis resentment. The analysis had entered the middle phase.

*

In the month of April, Rupert wrote down all his dreams—"the only thing I can write these days"—as fodder for his analysis. They were mainly comedic nightmares, visions of an audience telling jokes to a tongue-tied comedian onstage, a straight man who flicked cigar ash all over his partner's feet without feeding him any lines, or a gag writer who got stuck in a bathroom stall without any toilet paper and had to wipe himself with his own material.

"If I get a really funny dream, maybe I can work it into a routine," Rupert explained on the couch. "As it is, I'm not laughing much these days." He shifted position so he could look at the ceiling crack. "Tell me, what do *you* laugh at? What tickles your psychiatric funny bone?"

Dr. Blauberg passed a hand through his bald spot. His response was typical. "Why do you ask?"

"I like to know my audience, that's all. You know, you haven't said two words to me since Christmas."

Dr. Blauberg shifted uncomfortably in his chair. "What would you like me to say? Has something in particular been bothering you recently?"

Rupert gave a martyr's wave. "No, nothing, nothing. Only what would you do if you couldn't function anymore?"

"Go to an analyst" was on the tip of the doctor's tongue. He suppressed it. "Has the thought of what your father might think been troubling you lately?"

"What are you talking about? We've been over all this before. Son of a bitch never laughed in his life."

"I see."

"Well, I don't." But after the session, he went home and wrote a ten-minute sketch about an impossible father.

*

"What I want to know is, is it funny?" Rupert had just finished reading the father routine to Dr. Blauberg and was trying to elicit some sort of response. For once, Dr. Blauberg ventured past the realm of no opinion.

"Well, I don't laugh that easily. . . ."

"That bad, huh?"

"I find it more psychologically revealing than purely humorous."

"Great, so I'll read it to the New York Psychoanalytic Institute! How come it isn't funny?" He picked out a spot on the first page. "'Now I'm going to tear and father you'—maybe that's too clever."

"Well . . ."

"How about the snoring in Morse code? Or the part where the kid's told to get his own damn glass of water?"

"It has a lot of rancor, the whole piece."

"Oh, yeah?" He rose from the couch, and Dr. Blauberg began to fear for his replacement vase. "You know, I need to think through a few things," he told the psychiatric chair, and walked through the double doors. A ghostly "ha ha" echoed after him.

Rupert didn't return for over a week, and Dr. Blauberg decided to charge Rupert for the sessions he had missed. He had to watch himself: to get too interested in Rupert Schnayer's neurosis would be to lose all perspective, to become Rupert's audience. But after all, wasn't that what most patients desired—Mrs. Dowell, who sang occasionally to show what a fine soprano voice she once had, or Mr. Krupmeyer, who diffidently showed Dr. Blauberg his attempts at poetry?

Maybe he feels he'll be cured if he can make me laugh, he thought. He tried to laugh then, but it came out as more of an apologetic chuckle. He peered out the window of his tenth-floor office, waiting for Rupert to return.

*

"On long interstellar journeys, I frequently get speeding tickets."
Rupert, back on the Wednesday after, made no mention of his absence, but launched directly into a monologue. It had something to do with space aliens landing at 34th Street near Macy's, and the story took over fifteen minutes to unravel. Near the end, it was mostly just unraveling. Finally, Rupert interrupted himself—"stop me if I'm boring you." He glanced over at Dr. Blauberg, who was looking benignly at him like a father at his son's music recital.

"Well, should I go on?"

"If you like, yes."

Rupert sulked for the rest of the session, pawing occasionally at the couch as if he were trying to get at some secret hidden in the springs. The only constant sound was the sigh of the air conditioner. At the end of the hour, Rupert got up, saluted the doctor, and left. Dr. Blauberg wondered with just a tinge of worry whether he himself was losing his sense of humor, his detachment, or what.

*

For the next few weeks, Rupert brought in a monologue a day, always watching the doctor's face to gauge the effect, always leaving more and more disappointed, even when a particularly pungent line brought a chuckle. *Never succumb to the patient's desire for gratification*, thought Dr. Blauberg, and he kept a perfectly straight face when Rupert talked of one camel humping another.

Rupert knew a lot of joke-runs, and it took a while before he even slowed his pace. He ended one Wednesday with a particularly repulsive string of jokes about amputees. When he paused, there was dead silence in the office.

"Are you finished?" asked Dr. Blauberg, in what he hoped was a neutral tone.

Rupert looked surprised as always, as if he had put on an act to what he now saw was an empty auditorium. Only this time he stood up, staring hard at the doctor's chair. "What did you say?"

"I just wanted to know if you were finished." Dr. Blauberg felt he should clarify. "So we can discuss the impulse behind it."

Rupert cocked his head, as if to consider the question from all angles. He nodded determinedly. "Yes, I'm finished. For good." He took a brief bow and exited, stage left. A vacuum hung in the air, possibly to be filled by applause. Dr. Blauberg waited for several minutes, but Rupert didn't come back for an encore. As the days passed, it became apparent that he wasn't coming back at all. Two and a half years of analysis abandoned just like that, thought Dr. Blauberg. Tossed out like a routine that failed to get a rise.

*

I should have laughed at his jokes—should I have laughed at his jokes? After two weeks, Dr. Blauberg called Rupert's residence, a cheap studio apartment on upper Broadway, but no one was ever home, or at least no one ever answered. Twice he got an answering machine that told him, "Fabulous, fabulous! What'd you say your name was?" He left two polite inquiries. After a while, he gave up, even though the last check for four sessions never came. The bills he sent were returned, "ADDRESSEE DISEASED" scrawled in red on the envelopes. Soon, Dr. Blauberg had another patient to fill the space, a widower named Randower with a sexual fixation on obese women. Rupert Schnayer became another name pressing lightly on the doctor's conscience.

*

Six months passed without incident. Dr. Blauberg no longer checked under his seat for whoopee cushions, though he began to notice that some of his patients' outpourings were extremely boring. He wondered whether he shouldn't get out more in the evenings. It was on a rather dull weeknight in mid-February when he found himself at the Hot Spot, a sort of nightclub *cum* bar on Waverly Street. He was one of a handful of patrons. The next show wasn't until ten—it was open-mike night—and he had a gin and tonic while he waited. He felt obscurely uncomfortable and considered leaving.

But then it was ten o'clock, most of the other tables had filled up, and the stage lights went on. The emcee, an ectomorph in faded dungarees, introduced the show, then left the stage open. The first two hopefuls weren't up to much. One was a large man who delivered all his jokes as if he were walking into a strong wind; the other was a woman who kept glancing nervously around the audience. After they finished, there was a momentary lull. The curtain swayed, and the sounds of a scuffle could be heard from behind. With a clash of cymbals, an all-too-familiar figure sprinted onto the stage. He wore white tennis sneakers and a straightjacket with the straps tied tightly, and was straining to look back over his shoulder as if he expected someone to be chasing after him with a net. He looked wildly right and left, but the panic was clearly a pose. When he caught sight of the doctor's table, Rupert showed a newly confident presence. Then he launched into his monologue.

"A man walks into a psychiatrist's office, says, 'Thank you so much, doctor, I no longer think I'm a dog.' Psychiatrist says, 'Fine, so you're not sick anymore?' Man says, 'Of course not—just feel my nose!' Hey, how many psychiatrists does it take to change a lightbulb? Only one, but the lightbulb has to *want* to change. Two women are talking: one says, 'I'm worried about my Freddie, the psychiatrist says he has an Oedipus complex.' Other lady sneers, 'Oedipus-schmoedipus, so long as he loves his mother!' "

Dr. Blauberg rose from his seat, having found out what he wanted to know.

"A young lady falls in love with her psychiatrist; she says, 'Doctor, I shouldn't be kissing you, should I?' Psychiatrist says, 'Are you kidding? I shouldn't even be lying here on the couch with you!' Woman on the couch says, 'Doctor, every dream I have, you say it's phallic. What *is* a phallus, anyway?' Doctor stands up, unzips, says, 'This, my dear lady, is a phallus.' She gapes. 'Oh, you mean it's like a prick, only smaller!' " Rupert's manic laughter was punctuated with another clash of cymbals as Dr. Blauberg stumbled through the confusion of tables and chairs. The monologue was picking up speed. A ripple of laughter passed through the crowd.

"A surgeon and a psychiatrist in an elevator: the surgeon says, 'How do you take it, listening to all those problems every day?' Psychiatrist says, 'Who listens?' "

Dr. Blauberg cringed but did not turn around. He might have caught Rupert's eye, and he thought that such a glance would be disastrous—for one of them, anyway. A wave of laughter threatened to engulf him, and he felt the need for air. He pawed his way toward the exit. "But doctor, I can't swim, I—glub glub glub—" were the last words he heard before he passed through the double doors, toward comparative safety, into the hush of the night.

THE WEB OF MÖBIUS

I

THE CORRIDOR is divided into checkered squares, then vague rectangles of darkness, stretching to points of light. There are no openings or features along the corridor, and the measured tread of my footsteps is the only order present. Lately, I've been having the same dream over and over, with minor, frightening variations.

Last night, the Blood Lady came up to me during my walk, carrying a rose with ice thorns cupped between her hands. Since looking directly at her reveals that she has no head, I accept her rose while looking down at the checkerboard floor. After she is gone, the rose splinters into fragments, creating a puddle on the ground, which might be the ceiling or the wall. After this disturbance, the corridor slowly starts to fade out, the walls shrink inward, and transparent spots appear in the corridor, outside of which I can now see that it is blue night. The whole scene fades out. Then I fade out, too.

*

All I see nowadays is the blurred milky whiteness of sheets curled over the cot. When I look up, there's the white soundproofed ceiling, with little worm holes to trap the sound. The walls are white and the floor is beige and I lead an absolutely calm existence. I would like to wash my hands of the whole affair. Note: when I told this comment to Dr. Blodgeson, he said it proved I still had a sense of humor, though possibly dormant. I had to laugh.

*

During the day, I used to read, until the print began to wear holes in my eyes and the books wouldn't stay still. When they took *King Lear* away from me, it had blood and spittle stains all over it. Nowadays I spend much of my time in bed, looking at the worm holes in the ceiling. If I look at them long enough, they move, which is no surprise to me, since any fool knows the ceiling really doesn't *trap* the sound we make. Actually, there are little worms tunneling all around the ceiling. Every once in a while they make obscene gestures, which most people can't understand because they can't read what the worms say.

The worm story was told to me by Eklund, the man in the cot next to mine, who can read worm language. But not with his glasses off. When I took his glasses to find out how to see what the worms were saying, he said they would only work for him. Eklund is a very personalized person. He has his own Coke can and his own funnel. Whenever he gets enough money to buy a Coke from the red machine down the hall, he first pours it into his own can and lets it sit a while. He claims it saved his life once, and I nod solemnly.

The other cot next to mine is vacant and has been unoccupied for all the time I've been here. Eklund told me the last patient in it died, and another inmate told me that it's still occupied, so I don't know which of them to believe. On some days, I tell Eklund he is full of shit, and this turns him into an ice statue.

*

When I get tired of staring at the sky and counting worms, I rehearse what I know. Lately, the list of what I know has been increasing a lot, and it takes longer and longer to go over it all. If I let just one day, even one day, pass by without rehearsal, I will lose it all and have to start all over again. Yesterday I finally learned the ward nurse's name, which is just one example of all the facts I have to include. Her name is Cathy. The day before, someone told me another fact, that the sky was a deep, deep blue, but I said he was full of shit because the sky isn't blue at all. It is white, I told him, white with little worm holes all around. He looked at me as if I were crazy, which shook me up a bit. I am still recovering.

The few periods which break up the daily space are occasional meals and afternoon recreation. I can't remember the meals, but afternoon recreation takes place every day at two o'clock, which is any time, because it is really whenever Cathy says it is. Cathy. Cathy, Cathy, Cathy. I have to repeat it; otherwise it will slide away into darkness.

During our recreation, we all line up in the recreation room, which is a large blank space with a spot in the center where someone once ripped off a TV set with long antlers. We do a few exercises and then the nurse *Cathy* leaves the room and lets us play for a while. The most popular game is Duck, Duck, Goose, but the last time someone picked on Eklund he turned into another ice statue, so lately we have been playing Twenty Questions. It's a very easy game, since everyone always picks the same objects to guess at. When it was my turn, I picked the old disappeared TV set. But then nobody could get it, so they all got mad.

*

The only way to see time pass here is to watch for Incidents that come and go. Otherwise time doesn't pass, and it's like the white on the walls or the gray-green of the cots and it just stays there.

The last Incident was when the lady I-don't-know-how-many-cots-down started beating up on—Cathy, and she tore at Cathy's uniform and started clawing at her. The lady shouted and Cathy shouted and someone else came into the ward and separated them as if they were two little boys fighting. That's when I learned the nurse's name was Cathy. And I thought about what two little boys fighting looked like, since there are no little boys here, only inmates. This makes me think that some of my knowledge is remembered rather than created. It makes me feel less smart, but maybe I can remember more. It is slow work.

My question is how I got here, but I don't remember and I couldn't think of anything to make up. I think I'm waiting for something, but no one will say anything. Cathy pretended she didn't hear my question when I asked her, but later she brought me a book to read. It was bound in cardboard and said *Jungle Jim*. I wanted another book and I told her that, but nothing happened. When they took the book away from me, it was all wet.

At night, I've been dreaming the same dream recently, which is bothering me. The shapes in the other cots turn to ice statues and the corridor begins to form around me, down and up and sideways into infinity. I always walk alone and sometimes a red lady catches up with me and sometimes she doesn't, but I can never finish my walk before the tunnel starts collapsing and I never quite make it out. I wake up looking at the worm holes in the sky, and the white walls and the whiteness of it all. At times, in the middle of the night, it is very quiet.

II

Now I figure I may have been forgetting things, things I knew just a while ago but now they've faded into the white mist of the ward sheets. I *know* I used to know the last name of the ward nurse—

Cathy; she told me once, and now I can't bring it back, since I must have forgotten to rehearse it. Cathy Blank, Cathy Nobody, I wonder who you are.

Or maybe I forgot because there are too many facts crowding in my brain already. I learn something every day—that sounds familiar, too. A while ago another person came into the ward in a white suit. He said he was here to help, and under his bushy brown mustache he had a big red smile which he could flick on and off at the touch of a button. He smiled at me then and said I had to get back, pull myself together. At the time, I *did* feel as if many different parts of me were in corners of the ward, with my head dangling out the window. He made marks on a pad I couldn't read, and I'm beginning to think I can't read anymore. After he left, the—Cathy took an ice needle and stuck it into my arm, and the ice flowed through my veins and froze me. So far, she has done that seven times, unless I missed a few. When I asked her about it, she said *shh*, you're getting better. I'm afraid of the ice needle; it's too cold.

*

There was a shiny plastic design on the wall away from me for a while. It had a twisting face on it and a few colors. Then it just left, or it got ruined, because I remember seeing it on the floor with bite marks all over the sides, which made my jaw ache all afternoon looking at it. I went to sleep and the plastic piece was all bent when I woke up. I asked the gray man what happened and he leaned over and told me a horrible thing. They gave me something for my jaw at night and they put a bandage on the old man. So he'd stop telling me horrible things. They moved him away. The plastic piece isn't there anymore.

*

When I woke up this morning, I looked at the white sky. I looked down and I saw what wasn't there. Eklund was gone. They must have turned him into a statue again and carted him off during the night. His bed was stripped and the only thing left was his Coke can on the table. I knew it was his can because he had once scratched EKLUND on the side with a spoon. I fell back asleep again, and when I finally woke up, the can was gone, too. Cathy Raskin came by when she usually does to give me the needle, but I couldn't work up the strength to ask her where the Coke-can man had gone. I was afraid she'd tell me he never was, never breathed, never told me the sky was full of little worm holes etched in white. So I asked her when she would stop shooting me with shots, and she told me I was getting better.

And now it occurs to me that some things don't have to be rehearsed each day: I'll never forget the shots, I'll never forget Cathy Raskin's frost smile.

Please God don't let me forget Eklund.

*

Cathy smiled at me today and said she had a new form of therapy. I said oh, and she laughed and said don't be that way. She gave me some colored strips of plastic and a picture of a basket. She said I was supposed to weave the strips into a basket, look, *in* and *out*, and *in* and *out*, see? And I did sort of see, and in a few seconds I had a basket right under my fingers. But she said no, that wasn't the way to do it, oh what a mess, here let me show you again. I let her do half the basket that way; by that time I got the hang of it and finished it myself. Anyone can make a basket, and I don't know what they meant when they said therapy. When I finished it, they let me keep it on my table overnight. They took it apart and gave it to someone else in the morning.

They gave it to the old lady with the sad apple face. She started trying to weave the damn thing, with Cathy Raskin smiling at her, but she couldn't do it. She kept on turning the strips so they made loops with twists in them. Then she ran her finger along one loop around and around with no end and no beginning. But she started clawing at the plastic strips, so Cathy had to take them away from her. No one ended up having a basket, or even a brightly colored therapy.

*

Today is tomorrow now, but last night the red lady walked down the passageway to give me something. And when I held out my hands, she gave me a basket. And when I looked up she had no head. And I screamed. Cathy Raskin rushed in and tried to hold me down, but I told her no, no, please, I'm okay. She took her hands off me and backed away into the night.

When I looked up at the ceiling, I remembered what I told Cathy and I really wasn't okay. Maybe that's what made Cathy go away. Anyway, it gave me a good feeling that I'd gotten her not to use the needle, just by speaking at her. If I told her to come, would she?

Long after Cathy left, I looked through the glass wall behind the bed, where the night colors come through and crawl up the sheets. Sometimes they reflect onto the ceiling—and that night one of them looked like Eklund, Eklund writhing about in a mass of worms, with his glasses off.

I looked down into the blank of the sheets and made sure I didn't look up again, but I couldn't go to sleep. I was afraid Eklund would fall on me if I did.

*

Dr. Blodgeson asked me to describe the tunnel to him, but I could only wave my hands. Dr. Blodgeson is the chief ward doctor (Blodgeson, Blodgeson, Blodgeson) and he said he was interested in my case. I wonder if he's interested in me. But he wanted to know, so

I told him about the lady dripping blood, and she's got no head, and the corridor going clear blue with sometimes fish swimming outside. He smiled.

And I smiled back. So what.

Cathy came in during the afternoon and gave me a little yellow button with two eye-dots and a circle of a smile. I smiled and said it was very nice. When she left, I thought, I've never seen anything so stupid in all my life. I gave it to the gray man with the axe grin, who drooled on it and hid it in his bed.

★

I'm beginning to recall whirled-around events and people that I've never seen inside the ward. There's a lady with a gray coat and red, red lips, and a small dog that won't stop barking. I described a building to Dr. Blodgeson, and he said I must have been to Paris. The way he said it, Paris is a long way off and it is not white at all.

Talking with Dr. Blodgeson, I get the feeling that I'm traveling somewhere at high speed, and if I jump off I'll get killed. The corridor turned into a railroad tunnel two nights ago, and when the train had passed into ashes, I noticed the red lady's head was missing.

But then she turned around and smiled. . . .

★

The day after the smile, Cathy told me something during recreation period. While everyone was playing Twenty Questions, she came up to me, maybe just to hear me say hello Cathy, which I have been doing lately. I said hello Cathy.

She said hello Daniel.

And I was going to say who's Daniel when I realized she was looking at me. Only the woman in the pink nightgown doesn't look at you when she talks to you. Everybody else does, though. I rolled *Daniel* around on my tongue, and Cathy thought I had a piece of corn stuck in my mouth from the lunch food. I opened my mouth to show her I didn't. She liked that and went back to supervising the game. In two more questions, the lady in the pink nightgown got the answer—the old couch in the recreation room. It's the couch, she said, looking at the disappeared TV set. After a while, we all went back to the ward room.

Cathy brought me a book with gold letters on the outside. I told her I would be very careful, but she smiled her frost smile before she left.

The next day a new inmate filled Eklund's old bed, snoring. He was big and red with a crooked head and a low rumble, like a cat's purr. Except when they came to give him the ice shot, he threw up all over Cathy. I didn't laugh out loud because Cathy would have said I had no sense of humor.

*

The hallway comes to a point at the edge of the plane. I am sharp and angular and keep bumping my head on the ceiling, which lifts above me at times. It is blue and bulbous, with Eklund floating in the shade. The floor is littered with millions of personalized Coke cans, only one of which is his. The sides of the hallway turn clear when the lady in red comes down the path through the grass. She offers me a sharp scissors, which I take in my hand absentmindedly. I feel red and sharp, I take up the scissors and *stab her in the throat*. There is no face but mist, and when the mist clears away I see Nancy, bulging cheeks and brown ceramic eyes like a doll and it's Nancy it's Nancy it's my wife Nancy no it's Nancy. The scissors are back in my hand and I plunge—

into the white sheet. Something red whirls down the white sheet, and Cathy is standing beside the bed with a needle. She sticks me, saying it will be all right, but I don't even want to smile.

It will never be all right, and it will never be the same. I look at the white sky before falling asleep again, but Eklund has left. It may have been days ago.

*

I gave Cathy the book back today. I couldn't read it but it looked in okay condition when I returned it. I figure maybe if I imitate them they won't keep me here much longer. All of a sudden it matters, and I realize that the ward is not the right place. The old lady two beds down looks at me with insane eyes, chewing on toothless nothings.

*

The ward has gotten shapes and sizes, so that the end of the room draws off to a point of light and my hands stretch past the edge, where it is very dark. At night it is cold, cold and icy under the sheets, when Cathy came in the morning and froze me over, saying I wet the bed. I remember, I remember but I don't. When I screw my eyes tight against my mind, all I see is a slowly revolving cave, with mouth-pink walls and icicles. Cathy changed the sheets and left me with a smile. Sometimes I feel I'm walking somewhere, but the path leads around and nowhere, twisting back into itself like a ceiling worm. I hear the click-click of shoes on the floor and it's Cathy.

*

At night, I've been dreaming the same dream recently, which is bothering me. The shapes in the other cots turn to ice statues and the corridor begins to form around me, down and up and sideways into infinity. I always walk alone and sometimes a red lady catches up with me and sometimes she doesn't, but I can never finish my walk before the tunnel starts collapsing, and I never quite make it out. I wake up looking at the worm holes in the sky, and the white walls and the whiteness of it all.

But you know what? At times, in the middle of the quiet, in the center of the screaming dead eye black, when I've almost reached the end of the corridor, a shadow figure turns on its sleepy haunches and gives me a tremendous, heavy wink.

III

AND DWELT IN A SEPARATE HOUSE

THE SIDE TRIP is Jill's idea—God knows where she found the reference, but she's always looking up things like that: the world's largest hot dogs, authentic beeswax handicrafts, and now the last leper colony in the U.S., in a small town called Carville outside Baton Rouge. I could file a complaint—I'm a lawyer—but I know better. Jill does occasional travel writing, and this just has to be checked out. For the past week, we've been touring down south with no set itinerary except New Orleans as a destination. Soon after we arrived, though, Jill got impatient. The city was mobbed with conventional tourists looking at conventional sights. We left New Orleans the next morning under a graying sky just this side of rain.

Jill has put more money into this vacation than I have, so she gets majority voting rights. And since I probably love her a shade more than she loves me, I tend to give in more often. In any event, at times like these she becomes unstoppable: her liquid brown eyes become set, and she gets a determined hunch to her shoulders that may become chronic by middle age. Her hands are gripping the wheel as if made of the same molded beige plastic. We don't talk much, but then we rarely do. We just sort of fit together like two unequal jigsaw puzzle pieces. While Jill is driving, my job is to sit tight with the map and play navigator.

"So where do we get off this road?" asks Jill as she speeds by a Dodge pickup with two Dobermans yelping out the window. For the past hour, we've been heading west on Route 10, but the woman from the leprosarium mentioned something about a turn at a place called Gonzales.

"Soon, I think. Gonzales is about an eighth of an inch ahead." I point on the map.

"How long?"

"Ten minutes, maybe." By now I'm used to peering at dots posing as towns and the wormlike pink lines that connect them. I wonder what our own town, Mount Carmel, Pennsylvania, looks like on a map of this scale. How would it show that I live almost a mile away from Jill? What do we rate? I look up to see a sign for Gonzales flash by, and we take the next exit. There's supposed to be a tour of the facilities at 1:00, and it's now 12:45. After jouncing along a pressed-gravel road for a few miles, we pass into Iberville Parish, which means we're close. The scenery is mostly swamp grass and scrub oak, but a strange odor hangs in the air, like something that should be dead but is still moving around.

"That can't be from the leprosarium, can it?" Jill wrinkles her petite nose, looking almost girlish. She happens to be thirty-five, and I just turned twenty-nine, but most people think she's the younger one. I'm half-convinced the only reason she's older is that she was in more of a hurry. It's only now, she says, that she's beginning to develop caution. We take a turn onto a river road and, as if suddenly summoned, chemical refineries loom to the right like giant brains, fed by thick white tubing that seems to run everywhere. Innocent-looking clouds arise from smokestacks like artillery shafts. We shut our windows and finish the ride without talking. This morning at breakfast we argued about living together—I'm for it and she's not—and the tone of the discussion still hangs between us like a ghostly deterrent. I want to say something now, but as always I have to wait for Jill to open up. She has unpredictable interludes of frost, ending in sudden blossom.

About a mile past the refineries, we spot a sign: Public Health Service, Center for the Study of Hansen's Disease. "That's what they call it now," Jill informs me as we stop in front of a squat green guardhouse. "Leprosy has a bad name." A woman in uniform waves us on after we tell her we're here for the tour. The grounds look like an endless football field without any goals, marked at intervals by low-set white and beige buildings. We're told to drive ahead to the training center and sign in.

When Jill finally parks the car and kills the engine, a hush invades our ears. We've been driving for over an hour and a half, and the sudden silence is like a presence, as if it's been waiting all this time to get through to us. I put my hand on Jill's shoulder and work my way up to her neck, which often gets stiff from tension. But she shrugs me off, saying we'll be late. We get out, my big hands dangling uselessly at my sides.

The Public Health Service is a branch of the military, Jill notes, which must be why the training center has so many pictures of uniformed individuals on the walls. The man behind the counter tells us to sign the register, and our guide will be along in a minute. I like the fact that our names in the book are practically touching. Below Jill's address, I've simply placed ditto marks. Already seated by the register is a black-coated minister and his wife, who smile decorously at us. They must be the "Harmony, Arkansas" just above us.

At 1:00 precisely, a bulky woman in a pink cardigan joins us, followed by an old black man. He approaches us as if walking into a strong wind, his hands burrowed into the pockets of his thick brown jacket, up to his forearms. At first I think he must be another tourist, with his own reasons for wanting to visit. He looks us over, nodding several times as if to confirm something to himself. Then he suddenly announces himself as our guide. He says his name is Jimmy and asks if we're ready.

We all say yes, the clergyman's assent covering ours in a hushed sepulchral tone. The bulky woman hurriedly signs the register—I catch only the first name, Ruth—and the tour begins. We follow Jimmy single file up a flight of stairs, my paces measured so as not to step on the heels of Jill's Irish walking shoes. I often make minor adjustments like this since Jill insists she's already well adjusted. From behind me, I can hear Ruth panting like a polite steam engine.

We are herded down a hall and into what looks like an instrument room. There, instead of giving us an introductory lecture on the disease, Jimmy parks us in front of a video screen, nudges a button with his elbow, and says he'll be back when it's over. We are alone.

The film relies heavily on blue-and-yellow schematics and a kindly male voice-over. Apparently, leprosy is no longer a stigma (blue shapes covering yellow): it isn't infectious after the first stage, and in any event only about ten percent of the population seems susceptible (scant segment of yellow remaining). It's caused by a bacterium that deadens the skin cells, so that those afflicted can't feel it when they bruise, burn, or cut themselves (pulsating pattern). The ancient image of lepers—scaly skin, fingers falling off—is really secondary damage from numbness. Nowadays, sulfone drugs can control the disease (pulsating stops). The voice-over ends with a fanfare of trumpets and a diagram of a blue-green, healthy world—it's that kind of film. All of us will live happily ever after. The minister bows in benediction. Jill takes out a notepad she carries in her purse and writes something down.

The first real stop on the tour is the main hospital building, which houses various clinics and waiting rooms. Jimmy knows practically everyone there and nods continually. "They all treat me as a general nuisance," he smiles, happy to be in the way. He talks to us mostly in short, over-the-shoulder commentary. He reminds me of someone, though I can't think offhand who it is.

We get some general history of the place, which was established in the previous century and in some ways looks as if it stopped there. On the second floor, the hospital branches into long cement walkways that ride above the marshy ground and link the various buildings. The distances are so great that people actually bicycle along the corridors: as we walk, a nurse pedals past us, and in the foreground a man rolls slowly away from us in a motorized wheelchair. I once calculated the distance I travel back and forth to Jill's apartment at over three hundred blocks a week. As it happens, I end up visiting her more than vice versa. Occasionally I have dreams of a magic tunnel connecting us.

We walk endlessly down the leprosarium corridors, following Jimmy's energetic but crablike pace. The walkways were built in the days before air-conditioning and have screens to let in the air and the sun, but the sky in Carville is the color of cement, reaching all the way down to the stiff, wiry grass. Outside looks pretty much the same as inside. A dirty blue-green pennant in the courtyard dangles from a pole in the breezeless air. Finally we arrive at another building.

We see laboratories, medical offices, and patients in waiting rooms. None of the people looks desperately sick, but a few have bandaged-up limbs, and all of them wear an invalid look like a heavy overcoat. I don't know what it is exactly, but the idea that they're interned here gives them a different aspect from regular hospital patients. It's as if being ill in this way is a full-time job, with its own hours and regulations. But if so, it's a dwindling profession, and there are few inmates around.

The patients wave to Jimmy, but say little. I can't help wondering how they feel about us. Staring at them would be rude, but I'm not so sure about the other way around. In any event, after a brief interval both sides look down at the floor, except for the minister, who gazes toward the ceiling. In fact, the general torpor seems infectious, like a yawn traveling across a room. Our group eventually shuffles out. Seeing us drag our feet, Jimmy begins to make a joke of everything, from doctors who might saw you in half to patients who act like children. "And the waiting. You wouldn't believe it! We have more waiting rooms than patients."

"Well, now, isn't that something?" Ruth remarks. She says this at regular intervals. At one time she was training as a registered nurse, or so she says, though she doesn't mention what interrupted her. Just now she's alone, having left her children in her station wagon along with her husband when she discovered that no one under sixteen could take the tour. As she talks, she keeps washing her hands with invisible soap. She tells us that she's still fascinated by disease and has read many inspirational books on the subject of healing. She even recommends a few titles to Jill, who nods politely. There are times when Jill will roll her eyes at me or discreetly nudge me in the ribs, but not now. Instead, I see her jotting down occasional notes on her pad.

Since the leprosarium was designed as a self-sustaining community, it has a wide range of facilities, including two gymnasiums and a canteen-bar with a long Formica counter. There's also a television lounge, where a host of patients has gathered that afternoon. So many of the rooms are half-empty or unused that this is our first look at a full assemblage. They're mostly old men in ill-fitting clothes, about ten or so, settled around the room like guests staying too late at a party. A game show flickers on the screen, but few of them are watching. Two of them speak to each other in a language that seems to hold no recognizable syllables. Outside the room again, Jimmy notes that the majority are Vietnamese. So the U.S. can't produce its own lepers anymore and has to import them from Asia. I find this idea funny, but I don't think Jill would appreciate it, and anyway she's writing something down, so I remain silent. There are times when our entire relationship seems predicated on mutual withdrawal, which can all too easily degenerate into single isolation. This is one of my arguments for why we should live together.

Across the courtyard, the buildings look fully occupied, presenting such a marked contrast to what we've seen that Ruth asks about it.

"Oh, that." Jimmy shrugs an elbow. "These days they use some of the buildings for a prison. Minimum security. Some very respectable citizens there." He makes a joke about white-collar crime, then assures us that the prisoners are afraid of the lepers and vice versa.

There's an entire film auditorium mostly abandoned when cable television became available. The prisoners use it on movie nights. We stare at the empty gun-metal gray seats in silence. Beyond the auditorium is a huge ballroom, where Jimmy claims the patients hold gala dances. I try to imagine the festivities but can't quite. Then again, I don't dance myself. Jill said she'd teach me but hasn't got around to it yet. Ruth puts a hand on her broad hip. "Well, now, isn't that something?" she says. The clergyman pretends as if he's attending, but his mind seems to be elsewhere, his hands cloistered behind his back. His wife simply follows him. I feel for Jill's hand, which stays just out of reach. She says nothing, but bites her lip pensively. Sometimes she makes it a point to ask questions. I do, too, but more in the capacity of a prosecutor. We met when she came into the courthouse to fight a traffic ticket. It's been nine months so far. I wonder if she's thinking what I am: what it must be like to be a patient in this institution, and whether it's any better across the courtyard.

At the time the tour should be ending, Jimmy is still showing us around. We view the offices of *The Star*, the hospital newspaper put out since 1930. The tubby editor wears a green eyeshade and rests his feet on the desk in time-honored journalistic fashion, though one foot is missing. He cheerfully calls Jimmy a shill, and Jimmy cries, "Muckraker!" This seems to be a ritual exchange. We move on to the shoe lab, where patients are fitted for special orthopedic needs (such as missing feet). To Jimmy's chagrin, no one is there that afternoon. "Maybe they're all out on strike," he tells us. "That's good, we can help ourselves! If the shoe fits, wear it." His banter grows faster, his jokes more strained, as he senses that our interest is flagging. I can't quite understand why we have such an insistent guide, who seems mostly self-informed and almost self-appointed. When the minister's wife asks him something medical, Jimmy only shrugs.

A visit to the chapel, richly carpeted and paneled in mahogany, occasions a few polite questions on the part of the minister. At the back of the chapel is a stained glass window of Jesus healing a leper; in front is a pulpit big as a throne. In the middle are row upon row of empty pews. But in line with the rest of the over-accommodation, Jimmy then leads us to a second chapel, far more austere, with a bare skylight over the pews. This one, Jimmy jokes, is for atheists on Sunday. There's an inscription on the far wall that we pass right by, but which I return to read: "And King Uzziah was a leper to the day of his death, and being a leper dwelt in a separate house.—2 Chron. 26:21." The group has moved on, and I hurry to catch up. From behind, I can hear Ruth telling the minister's wife how she prefers the first chapel, and what a comfort her faith is to her.

After walking around for almost two hours, my feet are beginning to feel numb. We are in the leprosarium gift shop when Ruth decides to buy some baskets and beads, mostly, she explains, to placate her children still in the car. Jill and I wait in the concrete corridor while Jimmy hunts up someone to register the sale. It's dank and getting chilly, and just as I'm feeling cold and unloved, Jill puts her arms around me.

"Kiss me," she whispers, her eyes wide open. "I've never been kissed in a leprosarium before."

For a moment I hesitate, wondering what prompted her. The romance of short notice? The competing silence? Her lips are only an inch away, slightly parted. I gather her in. Just then, the group reemerges from the shop. We spring apart, reassuming positions like soldiers in twin sentry boxes. Ruth displays her souvenirs, including a plaited trivet that reads "Love Conquers All." "Now, isn't that nice?" she insists. It is clearly the end of the tour, and we head back toward the training center without further discussion. But something is still missing, like a clue in an unsolved mystery, or a piece from a pattern.

Along the gravel driveway, Jimmy finally takes his hands out of his pockets. The fingers are twisted as cedar roots, with several missing. "I've been here almost thirty years," he remarks as if he is the final part of the exhibit. "They released me a long time ago, but I don't feel comfortable anywhere else." He holds out his hands like burnt offerings, admiring them in the weak sun. Now I know who he reminds me of: a legless man in Mount Carmel who stands against the First National Bank like part of the building. I sometimes give him change when I pass him on the sidewalk. Both men have the same dependent yet proprietary air.

"Well, isn't that—" says Ruth, and stops there. During the pause, the minister gravely thanks Jimmy for the tour and shakes that gnarled hand. His wife flashes us a last smile whose effect departs along with them. "This has been something," concludes Ruth, and edges away politely until it's permissible to turn her back. That leaves Jill and me with Jimmy.

Jill clears her throat. "Don't you ever want to see other people?"

Jimmy grins and looks crafty. "Oh, I do. People like you pass through all the time. I show them around." He sticks his hands deep into his pockets and nods with assurance. "There'll be another group tomorrow."

All the way back to the car, Jill and I hold hands, gripping tightly. It seems entirely appropriate, entirely necessary that we do.

ALL CRETANS

HIS FIFTH DAY in Greece, seeking a refuge from the whitened bones of history, Harriman left the palace of Knossos tour early and seated himself at a *kafenion*, ordering an ouzo because it seemed appropriate. As a rising attorney on the run from a decaying relationship with a younger man named Ben who thought the world of his own cheekbones, Harriman had booked the Grecian tour in a hurry, eager merely to put distance between himself and the subject of his affections. In Athens, admiring a row of caryatids, he became grateful for the adage "You can't take it with you." On the ferry from Piraeus to Iráklio, he imagined he saw dolphins in the wine-dark sea.

But the alabaster statues of Greek youths stirred him, and he found himself reaching out mentally to cup the chin of a Ganymede type. A javelin thrower, frozen in mid-thrust, had Ben's supposedly unique facial structure. Where was the deceit behind the brow? he wondered—the malleable jaw that shaped itself around so many easy-sounding phrases like "Me, too" and "Yes, let's."

Duplicity, he decided, as he took the first sip of his overpriced drink, was a constant. Just one of the paradoxes of life. At eleven in the morning, few people were at the *kafenion*, which was half-tucked into an alley but blossomed onto the street in a bouquet of tiny tables. His unhandsome waiter—why were all waiters in Greece called Stavros?—had glided away a moment ago, bearing a tray of improbably dirty glasses. He took a large gulp of ouzo, which tasted like a licorice whip immersed in alcohol. Ah, well. When in Greece, and so forth.

As he stretched his legs onto the adjoining seat at his table, Harriman caught sight of a shabby figure stalking toward him. The man looked like some mountain fighter from the Greek war of independence, dressed in a fustanella and walking with a slight limp. Sensing some sort of hustle, Harriman instinctively turned away. Too late. Adopting the proximal Mediterranean stance that had made Harriman uneasy since the start of his trip, the man stopped at his table. They communed a moment in the light breeze from the agora. Up close, he looked more like a beggar. Does he want some drachma? wondered Harriman warily, his hand straying towards his zipped-up fanny pack. The Greek stared at him steadily, as if from the wellhole of centuries. His cheeks were shadowed with stubble and soot. After a while he leaned over and said in words that weren't quite English, "I am a Cretan." He smiled, showing a few yellow teeth, and added in a stage whisper, "All Cretans are liars."

Harriman started backwards. His reaction included a half-recalled memory of the famous paradox as it was recited to him at NYU Law. Had it been Kliegler in Contracts? He saw Kliegler in his habitual gray suit, lecturing with his arms thrust forward as if delivering a large and awkward gift. A Cretan declares in a court of law that all Cretans are liars. If he's telling the truth, then he's lying, and vice versa.

Or maybe it had been earlier. In college, a favorite course of his had been History of Western Thought, taught by a ferociously bearded humanist named Albin. The syllabus ran from Plato to Wittgenstein, with a general acknowledgement that something frightening had happened after the Enlightenment. Something to do with logic and God. As a lawyer, Harriman steered clear of paradox, preferring to impale defendants on the cusp of their own words, but something about the Cretan in front of him suggested the invitingly dark mouth of the Minoan labyrinth. Or maybe it was simply the ouzo on an empty stomach. Slightly drunk and more than ordinarily explorative, he felt like prosecuting this man.

Harriman considered the case before him. If the Cretan were telling the truth, then his words were a lie. On the other hand, if he were lying, then he also couldn't be making that statement. What now? He tried to attract Stavros's attention for a witness, but he was on the far side of the *kafenion*, clearing saucers from one of the tables no larger than a dirty doily. Meanwhile the Cretan, a goat's breath away, was waiting for a response. In his soiled white kilt and fez, he could have been a busker who'd hitched a ferry ride from Athens—or a *klepht* fighting the Turks alongside Byron in Missolonghi.

Never mind, thought Harriman, never mind. His thoughts were rolling around in his head like a fleet of overturned barrels. He had a sudden vision of Albin, topped by Ben's head, emphasizing a point on the blackboard with the *tic-tac* of his chalk stub. From some recess of his mind, perhaps the one marked "cross-examination," he mentally removed a sheaf and scanned it quickly. He tilted his head up abruptly, the Cretan watching him warily. "That's easy for you to say," he finally retorted. He rose triumphantly, almost knocking over his doily table in the process and incidentally making the Cretan move a step. He spread his arms Kliegler-style, forcing the Cretan backwards into a nearby chair. "Maybe Cretans sometimes tell the truth and sometimes lie."

The Cretan stared furrily at him, his aneloid lips moving soundlessly as if sight-reading Harriman's words. Warming to his case,

Harriman continued. "When you say that all Cretans are liars, you're lying"—now he gestured like an umpire declaring a foul— "but that's just in this boxed-up logic of yours. You could be telling the truth tomorrow." He made as if to check his watch. "You can fib or you can be honest. Just like anyone else."

This resolution of an age-old paradox didn't sit well with the Cretan, who scowled as if a miniature cyclone had twisted his face. He clearly treasured his uniqueness as much as he relished his role in logic textbooks. Rising to his full height (more a matter of presence than physicality, since he turned out to be short and scrawny), he snarled some indecipherable Greek imprecation and stomped away. His fustanella swished back and forth like the flounce of a dress. He eventually disappeared around the corner of a stucco building in a sepia cloud of dust. Harriman mopped his brow, resettled his tumbler of ouzo, and took a sip. For some reason, the liqueur now tasted better, less like candy dropped into resin and more like a proper drink. Perhaps he'd have another.

He did so, and since it was now lunchtime, he also ordered a hummus-and-pita concoction that came with a border of stuffed grape leaves. A crowd began to gather at the *kafenion*, including a few members of the tour who looked at him with vague resentment, the way faithful students regard a kid playing hooky. He smiled blandly, too drowsy to mind. After Stavros cleared away the dishes and returned with a white thimble of coffee, Harriman fell into a doze. His one dream was concerned with a living statue that took off its toga to reveal the words "CRETAN" tattooed on one buttock and "LIAR" on the other.

Harriman awoke with a jump as Stavros clattered some plates nearby. He squinted into the sun, trying to estimate how much time had gone by. Perhaps an hour, perhaps an hour and a day— how could he tell? He sat and drank his now-cold coffee, which revived him minimally. This time of year, the locust trees spread

their branches like supplicants, the Dikti mountains looming behind everywhere. The afternoon shadows lengthened until the
image of the *kafenion* on the pavement was a forest of heads from
one table imprisoned in the latticework chairs from another. Harriman doodled a bit on his red paper napkin: a mazelike diagram
but without a minotaur at the center. He thought about the palace
of Knossos from this morning: the intricate design of so many little rooms, from the courtyard to the sanctuary. In the museum of
Heraklion, a fresco showed an acrobat leaping a stylized bull, and
one of the hand-seals was decorated with a gorgeous frieze of two
goats copulating. How Greek, he thought, suffused with feeling
for a race that so easily combined sex and art. One of the women
in the tour had made a silly joke, and he'd left soon after. What
the hell—he'd catch up with them at tonight's hotel.

He sipped his coffee, alone if not entirely free, trying to make
the moment last.

*

Harriman got up to visit the filthy toilet adjoining the *kafenion*,
ending up back at his seat as if pulled by an elastic string. All
during the afternoon, people and objects had moved by him, from
an old man bent over a bicycle to a flock of birds dark against the
sky. He would move on, too, eventually. Meanwhile he felt oddly
impelled to remain right where he was, as if his table had become
the center of the universe. He contemplated sending a postcard
back to Ben, but couldn't think of anything to say. "Wish you were
here" was a cliché as well as a lie. Ben always caught him at that,
though Ben freely lied himself, as he often confessed. The problem
was one of trust, or maybe just the trickiness of words.

He ordered another coffee and, while he was waiting for it, saw
a familiar figure approaching. The man nearing Harriman in the
slanted light looked like another Cretan. He could have been the

brother of the Cretan who'd accosted him before, though he appeared more purposeful and older, or simply timeless. This man looked like a Cretan from antiquity, in begrimed toga and sandals. The *kafenion* by now had emptied out, and there was nowhere to hide. Stavros the waiter was impossibly still clearing away cracked saucers from the same table as before.

The Cretan headed straight for Harriman. He laid a hand on the braided wire arm of Harriman's metal seat. Here we go again, thought Harriman.

"*Ena,*" the man intoned, and from somewhere in the blue-eyed sky came a thunderous voice: "ALL CRETANS ARE LIARS." The tone was apodictic, like the *Fiat lux* from Genesis.

Harriman said nothing. Awed as he was, he was also waiting for the other shoe to drop.

"*Dhi-o,*" remarked the Cretan, and the celestial voice-over, that which cannot be argued with, boomed down again like rain on the unlucky, "THIS MAN IS A CRETAN."

The Cretan smiled and executed a delicate little bow, indicating polite insolence as much as "at your service."

"*Tria . . .*" he whispered, leaning forward so that his forearm brushed Harriman's in the hirsute approximation of an eyelash kiss. His breath stunk of old loaves and olive piss. "*I am a liar.*"

A beat of a pause. Harriman opened his mouth, started to say something, and paused again. If Cretans were liars and this man was a Cretan, then he couldn't have said what he just had. This contract was more binding. Where was Kliegler when he needed him?

Another beat.

The immanent pressure of a headache came from within his skull, radiating outward in almost visible waves of pain. This was not the same situation as before. Someone above had switched the rules on him. He turned his head sideways, his best thinking posture, but nothing occurred. Given the setup, he could find no way out. The Cretan's arm snaked around the rim of the chair, moving toward Harriman's second thimble of coffee, which was still half-full or already half-empty. The hairy fingers were almost at the saucer.

"But wait," Harriman protested. Think, think, he thought—as the history of Western logic raced by him. He saw Albin yanking at his beard, pounding the chalk into the board so hard that the piece broke in two. "The only way out," he recalled Albin concluding one lecture, "is the exit."

And there it was. He shook his head as he rose. "I never agreed to the premises." Though his left leg had fallen asleep, he tried to stand, staggering a bit. "Who knows that all Cretans are liars? In fact, who says that you're a Cretan?" Pawing clumsily at the man's toga, he parted the clothing to reveal a modern belt buckle in the shape of a bugle, and a designer logo on a pair of cutoff jeans. A light push backwards, and the man crashed into a nearby table. As the proprietor rushed forward from somewhere in the bowels of the *kafenion*, the exposed pretender stumbled away, muttering angrily. The hem of his garment brushed the cobblestones like a cross between a besom and a shroud.

The proprietor offered a cursory apology as Harriman returned to his seat. Despite his apparent contrition, his manner suggested that Harriman order something. An ouzo, then. Stavros was dispatched to fetch it.

Harriman sat back in his chair, his gaze fixed on the horizon where the locust trees merged into one continuous gray smudge. Flapping toward him was a feeling of finality, of having wrestled something, but to a standstill rather than victory. Had he really escaped? From Ben in New York, or a Cretan in Greece? What, after all, did travel accomplish?

He swiveled in his chair, but since his chair didn't turn with him, he merely pinced his legs against the table. Had he really left at all? If a man shot an arrow at one of those trees, how would it arrive at its destination? Zeno's paradox, courtesy of Albin again. At instant one, the arrow is *here*. At instant two, the arrow is *there*. Then so much farther, and so on. So at any given moment, the arrow is motionless, yet it moves. How does it progress at all through a series of static frames? Is time a fluid medium or a series of discrete points? Cretans are bad enough. "To hell with Zeno," he muttered, as he waited for his drink. "God damn all Greeks."

But the problem wouldn't go away. This was a far deeper dilemma than the man who accosted Harriman a short while ago, or the earlier man, unless he was the same man simply removed in time. Would he, Harriman, be the same attorney boarding Olympic Airways for New York next week? Would Ben be the same terribly attractive, damnably annoying beardless youth?

His ouzo arrived in a badly washed tumbler remarkably like the first. Stavros or his twin turned his back on Harriman and walked away. In that time, an endless procession of men could pick up a myriad of tumblers in an infinity of bars. One had already broken up with Ben, another had just proposed that they move in together, and a third had never met the man in question. The fourth started toward Ben but never reached him. The fifth embraced the sixth, while the seventh stretched out his empty hand toward infinity.

One, thought Harriman, I am an American. Two, all Americans are dreamers. Three? He picked up the glass almost absently but stopped just a moment, pausing at the precipice, the landscape blurring into the distance, his hand close to shaking, before taking the first sip.

THE WORK OF ART IN THE
AGE OF MECHANICAL
REPRODUCTION

PUT THE STACK of paper into the feeder, ruffle the pages so no edges poke out, set the copy indicator to 2, adjust to medium dark, and press START. While the Kodak 3600 was effortlessly duplicating the bearded man's thesis, Doria took a look at the smudgy gray thesis writer, who looked a bit like a copy himself, standing in front of the counter with both hands curled around a flattened folder. Behind him stood an elderly lady with pursed lips and a set look in her eyes, and behind her a professorial type holding his place in a book with one soft pink forefinger.

The plastic-cube calendar on the counter read "4/7/77." More particularly, it was a little past ten on a Monday, and already Doria was behind on the copying work that should have been done Sunday for those customers who had dropped off material on Saturday. Magazine articles, recipes, theses, musical scores, flyers, everything copyable was fed into the large receiving maw and twinned, or triplicated, or multiplied by a hundred. Their utility was questionable. Who needed two hundred copies of an announcement for a macrobiotic learning experience next Tuesday at eight?

The READY signal flashed the blissful orange of completion. Reaching to take out the thesis original, she noted the title: "The Animacy of Inertia in the Modern Novel." The bearded man stared at her behind his rimless glasses, as if waiting for a sign of some kind: a grateful publisher appearing from under the counter, or a small academic audience assembled for the reading of a chapter. Doria promised neither. Instead, she stacked the original and the two copies in the vibrating collator, tapping her feet while the pages settled. She took all three bundles and slid them over the counter.

"That'll be eighteen sixty-two."

The student dug into his jeans. "That's a lot."

Doria shrugged. "You had a lot of pages. Next?" Marvin the acting student would be coming in at ten-thirty. In the meantime, she had to run a seamless operation, getting X's change while accepting Y's manuscript, keeping a steady flow of customers. This particular branch of KopyKat was in a good location, always busy. Since Doria had started three weeks ago, she estimated conservatively that she must have copied nearly half a million pages.

The old lady behind the student wanted a copy of an article from a book on gerontology. She called Doria "dear," the corners of her mouth emphasized in lipstick and vaguely twitching. She balked at the price for bound originals, but by then Doria had already made her copies. She stood there with the pages in her hand, the lady across from her shaking her head. "If you don't want them, I'll throw them out."

The old lady looked crafty, her mouth crooked. "If you're going to throw them out, then let me have them for free."

Doria sighed. It wasn't contempt, just frustration at dealing with people: with poets who wanted to pay for their copied verses in promised posterity, with businessmen who made duplicates of everything they read in a day. Now, if *she* had something to copy—but Doria had nothing she thought worthy. She looked hard at the woman, who clutched her handbag like a vestige of respectability. "Do you want the copies or don't you?"

The lady drew herself up. "No, thank you." She walked out, carrying her handbag in front of her.

Doria faced the next customer, the professorial type who wanted a copy of everything from pages 67 to 119 inclusive. The book was some kind of philosophical monograph, dense footnotes giving a two-toned appearance to each page. While the man waited for Doria to do what seven monks might have spent three years at, he took out a memorandum book and importantly crossed out items. After that came a man who wanted three tax returns, a girl with a term paper, and a Girl Scout troop leader who needed a hundred copies for a mailing. After the Girl Scout woman—something about a Cookie Drive—Marvin arrived, wheeling his ten-speed through the front entrance, flashing her a histrionic hello. He had on red pants with black cuffs, and a "Thespians Unite" T-shirt. It took him about five minutes to settle down behind the counter, but Marvin was all right, Doria had decided. In the worldview that Doria was quickly adopting, that of copies and originals, Marvin was an original. When Marvin started waiting on the line of customers, Doria took a cigarette break in back.

She blew a plume of Camel smoke toward the flammable solvents stored over by the copy paper. The past few days, she had felt the job getting to her, not just the pressure of crowds or the repetitive work, but the very act of copying others' material. Re-created images of short stories, résumés, letters . . . the quantity of it all irritated her, though she wasn't quite sure why. Occasionally, she ran across something she regarded as worthwhile: a safety notice, a hilarious cartoon, a scene from a play she had time to skim (the playwright had yet to pick up his copies). Far more often, it was drek. She looked around the walls of the storeroom, the steel shelving piled high with quires of copy paper, all destined to be turned into sterile reproduction. And she was one of those designated to help the process. It was depressing and she didn't want to think any more about it right now. She stubbed out her cigarette and returned to the counter.

With Marvin working at the small Xerox 240 in back, the line diminished, and disappeared altogether around eleven. The last customer was a heavyset man wearing a plaid shirt and overalls. He wanted five copies of the page he laid flat on the counter, watching to gauge her reaction. Doria, who had become quite skilled at reading upside down and sideways, studiously avoided both the paper and his gaze. She pressed it against the glass paten and set the machine for five copies. Meanwhile, the man fidgeted, placing one hand on top of another like a pink sand castle. He looked at her, looked away, and smiled a secret smile. When she came back with his copies, he urged her, "Go ahead, read it."

"Oh, that's all right, I never read the customers' material." An excusable lie. "Here, that'll be twenty-seven cents."

The man drew himself up. "I'm a very fine poet."

"I'm sure you are." She looked around for Marvin, but he had stepped into the storeroom for a moment.

"So go ahead, read it."

"I told you, I really don't—"

"*Read.*" He placed a hammy hand over her wrist, guiding her hand over the six identical pages. So she read. It was either read or step back to call the police, and it wasn't worth the risk. Keep the customer happy. So she read the poem, twenty lines or so of free verse, stumbling pornography about his second wife. Doria was no poet, but she did have an appreciation for poetry, which this wasn't.

She nodded. "Um, very nice."

The man nodded back eagerly. "I wrote it at one sitting. I write all my best stuff that way. That woman Yvonne, though, that's a made-up name."

"Oh?" Thank God Marvin returned just then. "Well, it's been

pleasant talking with you." She wrenched her hand away and darted back to the storeroom, with its comforting white boxes as barriers. She felt bruised and curled up against a carton of legal-size paper. It was an odd kind of solace, but the sheer bulk was momentarily reassuring. After a while, she just looked up at the white acoustical ceiling tiles, which were uniform in a nonthreatening way.

It was the renewed hum of the Kodak 3600 that brought her back to the counter. By that time, the poetry man had gone, and she realized that she had never collected his money. She put on a tight smile: doing her bit to help the arts. When she told the story to Marvin, he nodded sympathetically.

"I know what you mean. I had a lady in here the other day, wanted me to proofread her memoirs. 'The Reminiscences of a Kept Woman.' " Marvin rolled his eyes, batting his long lashes. "Copy shops are magnets for kooks. The only thing to do is turn the job into a game." He executed a heraldic flourish when he handed over the next customer's copies, to show what he meant. Doria nodded thoughtfully and took the next in line, a fat lady with a recipe for fudge.

The day ended at five, when a cadaverous man named Mahoney took the next shift. KopyKat's motto was "We're here when you need us," and it demonstrated that by staying open until midnight on weekdays, nine on weekends. But by six, Doria was thirty blocks downtown, making a kind of ragout in a pot for her supper. She shared a third-floor walk-up with a woman named Evelyn, who did office temp work, but who was currently on extended vacation somewhere in New Jersey. The half-empty apartment gave her more room for contemplation, she found. Now, she stirred the mixture of eggplant, mushrooms, tomatoes, and chicken while thinking about the process of copying, in general. During her three-week tenure at the store, she had yet to make a copy for herself. Of course, she hadn't produced anything. On the other hand, how convenient if she could copy her whole dinner for, say, next Saturday. Or would there be something immoral— here she tested her creation and blanched—in avoiding the work of cooking? In any event, she needed to improve the recipe.

She had better get used to her job, she knew. It was good employment for someone in New York who wasn't a rising success or even someone with keenly trained ambitions. Doria was twenty-six and had no pretensions of becoming a scholar, a dancer, a business mogul, an actor, a lawyer, or a writer. She had a distinct sense of self-worth, but it applied to herself, not to what she might do. What was there to copy? She felt that she, Doria Hansen, was precious, without the trappings of writing poetry or being the head of a committee on, say, Marxist doctrine. A man had come in the other day to copy a pamphlet on Marxist committees, in fact, a man who was growing a Leninist beard and a Khrushchevian paunch. He had pounded the counter emphatically. Really, the things people copied were such transparent casings for the people themselves, it was pitiful. People who wanted to duplicate their egos, and it was all such cheap goods. What gave them the right to copy so much mediocrity?

The complaint was in her mind the next day, as she made eleven copies of a student's short story for a creative writing workshop. She knew it was slated for that purpose; she saw the heading at the top of the first page, along with a signature—to prove authenticity? The author, a disappointed teenager with the wispy beginnings of a mustache, had also copyrighted his story, she noted, misspellings and all: "'Monsters,' all writes reserved, by Gordon Fletcher." He placed all the pages into a thick folder which presumably contained other efforts, multiplied and disseminated.

Doria thought about writing a short story herself, but the idea was absurd. She didn't write, and that was that. On the other hand, she was a discerning reader, and what gave these other people the idea that they wrote? Somehow, the idea of copying one's work removed all doubt: beating down the fear of failure through sheer force of numbers. Eleven copies gave a certain sense of solidity, if nothing else.

She had no more time to philosophize. The woman to follow tendered a résumé which specified that she was looking for an employer with warmth and charm, who would understand her creative talents without exploiting her. Twenty copies advertising the woman's creativity—Doria felt it was a waste of paper. These were unwholesome thoughts for a worker in a copy shop, and she told Marvin she was taking her lunch break early.

He nodded, looking back at her without faltering, feeding a thesis-length stack of pages into the Kodak machine. An alienated graduate student, or someone very like an alienated graduate student, waited in front of the counter, his fingers gripping the Formica edge as if the shop, and maybe his thesis along with it, were rocketing away from him. The thought suddenly entered Doria's head that she would be doing everyone a favor if she yanked the paper out of the machine and torched it. The image she saw, the copies being destroyed by beautiful, flickering flames, was only momentary, but it shocked her. She apologized to the customer, who accepted her remark as if people regularly apologized to him for no reason. Doria went out to lunch and spent the greater part of an hour looking at her reflection in a Dunkin' Donuts cup of coffee. I am an original, she reminded herself, but she couldn't take much comfort from the fact. The gum-chewing counterman who served her was obviously a clone.

The thought of going back to copy again dropped from impossibility to something distasteful, and finally feasible. By one o'clock, she had recovered sufficiently to be on hand for the next batch of customers, out on their lunch hours, using their time to duplicate.

Marvin went in back, munching on a jam-filled donut she had brought back for him.

Her first customer of the afternoon was a man wearing a shoe-string tie with a coral clasp. He had a plumped-out briefcase and ordered copies as if the counter were a buffet: ten pages from the little white book, three helpings of an already-copied article, one each of what looked like light verse, and a strong black outline to end. He stuffed it all into the throat of his briefcase. Doria felt like tossing a handful of paper clips after his retreating figure as garnish.

Time passed: more people, more copies, copies of copies, fifth-run copies, where the print achieved a grainy boldness from over-duplication, the original probably moldering in a sub-basement library shelf. This time, Marvin was out, unable to cheer her up.

She was handling someone's index cards—why not copy one's doodles, one's suicide note?—when she felt a surge of nausea pushing at her throat. The nausea reached her head, making her dizzy; she saw a flurry of white pages, copies stretching before her in a dizzying parade. She had to sit down, but there was no chair, so she leaned against the feeder, her arm resting across the glass of the copier as she tried to clear her head. The machine hummed along in sympathy. The dizziness left her, but the whiteness remained in the back of her mind. She shook her head a few times.

"Miss? You okay?" The customer attached to the index cards leaned over the counter. Was he anxious over her or his cards?

"I'll be all right." She took the latest copy from the out-tray and was about to put it with the others when she noticed that it was a copy of her arm. The copier had caught perfectly the crook of her elbow, the short, delicate forearm shading into grayness, cut off at the wrist. A mistake: she was about to throw it away when something about the arm, just the fact that it was hers, made her save it. She put it aside and finished the last of the customer's notecards. It was almost quitting time for her, and when she left, she took her copy with her. On the downtown bus, she held the paper at varying distances, upside down and sideways, too. It was a graceful arm, in good contrast. She wanted to show it to Evelyn, but Evelyn was still away, so Doria had to admire it herself.

The next day, she brought home a hand.

She had tried five different placements on the glass to get a good copy. The result was an outstretched palm, distinct at the whorls of her fingertips but shadowy, almost menacing, at the edges. It had presence. She dated it and hung it up in her room.

In the days that followed, she tried her face, a luminescent death mask with her nose squashed flat. Then her hair, seaweed strands merging into a black tide on legal-size paper. And finally when no one else was in the shop, her left breast, which came out all wrong, disappointing. Apparently, her body parts were not equally photogenic.

But the hand had been beautiful. She saw it every night before she went to bed. It beckoned to her, and sometimes she saw it during the day, as well, when she was making anonymous copies for other people. After a week of quiescence, she succumbed and went back to making hands. She had neat, tapering fingers with strong thumbs. For some reason, other people's hands didn't interest her.

She first experimented with placement, finding the sharpest focus not in the exact center but some three inches upwards. As for the hand itself, she began with knuckle balls and crossed fingers. During the next week, she tried gloved hands, naked fists, even trick amputation shots with the index finger mysteriously missing, but eventually she returned to her original concept. The powerful calm of the outstretched palm she found most compelling. From her experimental period, she saved a multiple-copy forest of branching fingers, and a blurred fist.

The flat hand became the invariant; she began to manipulate other variables. Too much pressure on the glass created obvious tension, as well as darkness. But lightness was partly an evasion. For one whole day, she tried montage backgrounds of customers' rejected copies. It was a question of finding the proper context. She discovered how to create swirling fields of gray by yanking the cover off the during the copy process. She got to work early, and by eight-thirty the waste basket was lined with hands. She moved through the rest of the day with an artist's smile of self-complicity. Marvin saw what she was doing and in a gallant gesture rescued a reject hand he particularly liked.

"Portrait of the Artist as a Young Hand," he dubbed it, and he predicted a brilliant career for her. Doria didn't mind the fun, but she was no exhibitionist. Her hand was hers alone.

Six days later, when the pressure and placement were right, and all the aleatory factors conspired in her favor, she pushed the START button and came out with a perfect hand. Its flawlessness was so apparent that she gave a small gasp as it slid into the out-tray. Each digit seemed to possess an identity of its own, strong and defiant against a pellucid gray backdrop, yet part of the quintessential whole. The lighter bands at the finger joints lent the drama of character. Staring at the whorls in all their detail was like getting lost in some maze where time had ceased to exist. She admired it for as long as she dared, then slipped it into a folder behind the counter. All day, she serviced customers, buoyed up by her accomplishment. That night, she brought it home and drank half a bottle of Burgundy to celebrate.

The glow lasted a few days. But the next week, she was faced with a depressing realization. To have created was admirable but not enough. She had achieved a masterpiece of sorts and had nowhere to go from there. She had neither the energy nor the creative vision to step toward higher achievements. Her artist's smile shrank to pursed lips, and the time passed like one long overexposure.

Marvin tried to jolly her out of her funk by copying the lyrics from an old Ian Dury and the Blockheads song, "Reasons to be Cheerful." He improvised a truly rancid set of puns all based on the word *hand*, but he couldn't break through the fixation. During the following weeks, Doria tried switching to faces, but she quickly realized she wasn't a face person. She returned briefly to experimentalism, but the success of her perfect model had ruined her for tricks. She went back to making others' copies and waited for something to happen.

And waited some more. It was a drizzly Thursday, and the raindrops hung from the store awning in intriguing catenaries, but still all that was on Doria's mind were hands. Or rather, the perfect hand, which was hanging in a frame at home in her room and which she didn't know what to do with. She wanted some instruction.

Just then, a woman in an orange raincoat came dripping in, laid a blurry page on the counter, and demanded seventy copies of whatever the hell it was. For the first time, Doria displayed the contempt she felt. "Why in the world do you want more of that?"

The woman, oddly enough, didn't seem offended. "Well, it's *finished*. Now, all I have to do is copy it." As Doria nodded in surprise, the woman pressed home her point. "That's what comes next, right?"

The sense penetrated Doria like dream-words. She nodded slowly during the copying, as if she had just received a directive. By mistake, she ran off eighty copies instead of seventy, but told the woman to keep the extras. "More is more," she explained, and the woman humored her with a smile. The next day, Doria took her hand out of its frame and brought it back to the shop in a plastic envelope.

The day after that, Doria brought home another perfect hand. She hung it up on the wall next to the one from the day before.

The day after that, Doria brought home another perfect hand. She hung it up on the wall next to the one from the day before.

THE INNER CHILD

WHEN HIS WIFE telephoned and told him not to wait up for her—the fifth time that month—Morgan was nonplussed. Diane was calling from Houston airport, the PA system slicing into their conversation like an uninvited third party. "Look, Morg—*now arriving at gate 6B*—hasn't been easy, but it's not as if—*please proceed to baggage area number 3*."

"I understand," said Morgan, who didn't. The nagging pain that he'd felt in his chest all day gave him another striated stab. He was holding the receiver like an unwashed piece of underwear, the responsibility for the cleaning of which was all his. He also handled most of the cooking, washing, and childcare. Their mutual son, Alex, was now four years old, with Morgan as the housedad. Diane was more the executive take-charge type, and what she chose to control was more in the line of high finance than high chairs. A rising star at a biotechnology corporation called Halcom, she believed that raising a child in the nineties was no longer a labor-intensive operation. That evasion was all right with Morgan, who'd quit a perfectly reasonable job as a sociology professor in order to bond with his son.

"You're a fool to give up tenure," his ex-colleagues had warned him, all of them firmly ensconced in an educational system that threatened to collapse from lack of funding.

"So long as you're happy," said his mother, now happily deceased.

"I think this is a good thing," Diane told him. "A boy needs his father."

"*Iggghoo*," Alex remarked at the time, his mouth crinkled up at the corners, his tiny hand clutching a wooden spoon. And that settled it.

The first year wasn't so much hellish as surreal. There was simultaneously no time and too much time—dishes to be washed, diapers to be changed, bottles of formula to be warmed up, errands to be run, cooking to start—yet no particular order in which to do all these activities, no progression of hours but body time, until Diane came home late in the evening, redolent of what Morgan termed attar of executive. Though she was only 5'3", corporate power seemed to make her taller, and she wore blue suits with shoulders like a linebacker's. When Halcom went multinational, Morgan imagined her astride whole continents. She'd always been sweetly assertive—she had the gift of making a request seem like a favor—but usually with a humorous touch, a wrinkling of her nose or a flyaway hand gesture. As the obligations of her job grew, her Cupid's bow lips compressed to a hard line. "A little cooperation is what's needed," she'd mutter, even to Alex mewling in his crib.

Meanwhile the world seemed to recede further and further away from Morgan until even the small liberal arts college where he'd once worked seemed on a different planet, the word *sociology* coined by a distant race of superior beings. When he found himself in adult company, he often talked in a strange hodgepodge of semaphore and pidgin English, like a nineteenth-century Britisher left too long in the bushland. Some days, shopping was as close to civilization as he got. At other times, all he had to console himself with was Alex's carved wooden rattle, thrown under the settee, which Morgan retrieved and waved around like a castanet while watching *Sesame Street*.

"*Iggghaa*," gurgled Alex at his silly father.

"Alex made a new sound this morning," said Morgan to his wife that night. There was chicken stir-fry in the wok on the stove, but Diane had already snatched a bite before grabbing the shuttle from Kennedy. Trying to shed the same five pounds she'd lost twice last year was making her self-conscious about what she ate.

"Really? Tell Mommy." She lifted her son in the air, holding him at arm's length so as not to stain her red Armani suit.

"*Iggghaa*," said Alex, wiggling all his fingers at once.

"You said that yesterday, darling."

"*Iggghee!*" he insisted.

"All right, who's Iggy? An imaginary playmate?"

"I think it means he's happy," said Morgan.

"Well, good." Diane leaned her face forward, peering hugely at her son. She tickled him until he squirmed. "Happy, we happy, are we happy yet?" Finally she handed Alex over to her husband. "So how was your day?"

"Same." Morgan absently rubbed the sweet spot on Alex's stomach. "Yours?"

"Busy as hell. Meetings all morning, lunch with the Dryskin Group—big, big licensing agreements. Number crunching and phone work all afternoon. This better be leading somewhere, is all I can say." She yawned behind a well-manicured hand. Then, in a small voice that Morgan recalled as if from an earlier life, she asked him to massage her back. As Morgan eased the stiffness from her hunched shoulders, she reached out to pretend-massage Alex.

"*Iggghaa . . .*" he cooed. "*Iggghoo, iggghum. . . .*"

At ten months, Alex uttered his first word: "Mama." Morgan was at first crestfallen, but put the best face on the situation, making a tape of it for when his wife got back from a business trip to Tokyo. "The sound quality on that machine has always been bad," she commented when she heard it. "We should've bought a Sony." She turned to Alex, already dressed for bed in his Alex Duck pajamas. "Say it again, darling—let's hear you say 'Mama.' "

"Mama," declaimed Alex, his arms outstretched to Morgan.

"You," she accused her husband, "have some explaining to do."

Yet after Alex went to sleep, the bickering soon tapered off, not into agreement but silence. Some nights their most prolonged encounter was in bed, when neither felt much like talking. Diane still relished every inch of her body stroked, and Morgan enjoyed doing it, drawing his long, sensitive fingers from her cute instep to the hairy whorl at the exact top of her head—and four inches below her navel. Sex itself remained an enticing prospect, an indistinct figure dancing naked to an ever-diminishing point on the horizon.

Worrying about Alex, Morgan also fell prey to insomnia. Late at night, even after a satisfactory bout of lovemaking, he would creep into the darkened kitchen and help himself to a handful of his son's animal crackers. No tigers or lions were left, since those were Alex's favorites, so Morgan would console himself with a seal or an elephant. *Milk*, he added to the shopping list in his mind. *And Cheerios for Alex's breakfast.* His dreams were often filled with headless teddy bears and sword swallowers with faces like Diane's.

"You toss and turn a lot," she complained.

"You steal the sheet and wrap it between your legs."

So they got a bigger bed with a firmer mattress. Alex loved to bounce from one side to the other.

"One-two-three, *boing!*" cried Diane.

"Careful—you almost fell off the bed that time," warned Morgan.

As Alex progressed to the Terrible Twos, he would stomp around the living room in his new blue Velcro shoes, trying to make the television shake hard enough for the precariously propped-up remote control to hit the floor. He looked like his father, with the same smooth profile and curly dark hair, but acted more like his mother and loved to bark out orders on a red toy telephone that Diane had brought back from one of her business trips. "Hello, this Alex," he would tell the receiver. "Who there?"

"I can't get him to eat anything but peanut butter and Ritz crackers," complained Morgan one evening. It had been what he called a chasing day with Alex.

Diane folded her arms and said in a tone that was a tricky blend of indulgent and negligent, "Let him eat cake."

Morgan shook his head wildly. "We don't have any cake in the house, and I don't think it's a good idea to—"

"*Joke*, Morg. It was just a joke."

"Oh."

"Do I look like Marie Antoinette?" She tossed her head, tilting her nose Gallically.

"Let's see. That would make me Louis the What?" And he gave her a long French kiss. She reached out to hold onto his shoulders. The embrace melted into the best sex they'd had in a year.

Still, Morgan stopped asking her about the proper baby shampoo for Alex's itchy scalp, or the best way to get Alex to stay still while changing his diaper (imitate an airplane zooming down from an imaginary cloud). And though he moved on from the old alligator-to-zebra picture books, he never stopped reciting from the pages of Dr. Seuss because he'd read in an issue of *Parenting* that rhyme helped children make connections.

Morgan's own father had read a lot, but mostly the *Daily Post* behind a cloud of cigar smoke. A heart attack had carried him off when Morgan was five, and so he remained frozen in that image, growling from across the room for someone to get him another glass of seltzer. His mother was stretched between a secretarial job and two children, always slightly out of breath and running late. "It was never easy," she told him at the end, "but it was sometimes fun." Early on, Morgan determined not to growl at Alex and to try making it enjoyable. In fact, he was occasionally envious of the treatment he gave his son. Diane's parents were alive but distant.

It always came down to one thing, love of Alex. Over the course of his son's short lifetime, Morgan estimated, he had changed over five thousand diapers. The early-morning risings, the flung food, the blithe indifference to authority—all could be forgiven for a reached-out hand small as a starfish, and a pair of blue eyes that questioned the necessity of baths, naptime, and broccoli. He crouched to be on Alex's level, and often fell asleep while Diane was away by slowly rocking in the chair inside his son's bedroom. At times, he dreamed he *was* Alex, and he would wake with an almost intolerable joy that his whole life was ahead of him. If upon waking he discovered that much of it was behind him and that he had grown into a stooped-over adult, at least there was Alex, always ready to play.

Yet Alex still rushed for his mother whenever she arrived home, often bringing a toy like a board game that Morgan knew was age-inappropriate. "Diane, he doesn't know how to play Parcheesi." Morgan looked at the big box, wondering if he could return it for a dozen rubber ducks. "He can't even add numbers yet!"

"He can learn." Diane looked at him closely. "Honestly, Morg, sometimes I think you're too protective."

"Meaning what exactly?"

"He needs room to grow."

When Halcom expanded its operations to southeast Asia, Diane had to leave for a month. She called it her guilt trip. "I'm going to miss the hell out of both of you," she told father and child as she climbed into a black Fleetwood company car headed for Kennedy. She called most days, along with sending an occasional humorous note.

"Look, Mommy sent this to you," Morgan showed his son. Underneath the large Halcom-company logo were two scribbled lines:

Dear, I love you to the max,

So I thought I'd send this fax.

It was signed "Chief Coordinator of Mommy Operations," and Alex made Morgan read it aloud three times.

"What's 'cordator' mean?" he asked, his wide cartoon eyes suddenly worried.

"It means she's trying to do a lot of different things at the same time."

"Oh." Alex pondered for a moment. "Why?"

Because that's the definition of parenthood, thought Morgan. To Alex he simply replied, "Because she's busy. Now let's go outside."

Morgan found a new playgroup in the local park and spent his mornings on a wooden bench, bobbing his head between a glimpse of the newspaper and a view of Alex on a safety swing. Soon after Diane came back, she was promoted to executive vice president, which theoretically meant she could relax a bit, though practically speaking it meant that she came home earlier but brought her job with her. Taped to Alex's little maple-wood desk was a flowchart she let him have. He adored the diagram, tracing the multitask steps over and over. She taught him the word *efficiency*, which he pronounced "fishy sea."

When Alex was three, Diane decided it was time to send him to the Funnybrook Daycare Center. For a while, the centers of Morgan's days were faceless as a pack of blank index cards. He wandered through the empty house, wondering what to do with his time, preparing a lot of elaborate lunches that went half-uneaten. Passing into Alex's room, he guiltily patted down the fire-engine bedspread, as if to draw some essence of Alex from the fabric. During a spare Saturday, Diane had picked out the decor for the room, in which every object resembled something else: the small wooden chair was painted like a giant beetle, the bed was shaped like a Ferrari, and the game chest closed like a giant mouth over a considerable amount of loot, including the Parcheesi set and a Scrabble board gathering dust.

The rocket trajectory of their lives was changing course again. Diane began coming home later again, occasionally staying away even during weekends. When she was alone with Morgan, they were shy almost to the point of lunacy. Once when they hired a sitter so they could go see a movie, Morgan felt like asking to hold Diane's hand. At the park he was almost seduced by a mother in cutoffs whose little girl had taken a liking to Alex, but he fled with his son and later wondered why.

Diane has her job, and I need one, too, he decided. He went through his old syllabi, thinking of teaching again, but the academic job market had become a precarious cliff over which applicants leaped and dashed their skulls on the shoals of interviewing committees, the sheer number large as that of a lemming horde.

"You should try a career-counseling service," suggested Diane. And so Morgan found himself on the wrong side of a kidney-shaped desk, talking to a man in a turtleneck and blazer about employment.

Before Morgan could get very far, the man held up a hand. "First take these simple tests," he said with an obviously practiced cheeriness, sliding over a sheaf of papers to Morgan's side of the desk. "You never know what you might be good at till you try."

Morgan dutifully worked his way through a battery of aptitude tests with questions like "Johnny has nine cans of tuna, each costing 63¢. If Johnny gives three cans to Mary, how much money in tuna does he still have?" *Tuna is Alex's favorite lunch*, thought Morgan as he did some quick multiplication and subtraction, *but the last time it cost 63¢, I was still in school*. He also performed some executive decisions—"Which of these individuals would you fire?"—and manipulated colored rods to make a pleasing pattern on a three-dimensional grid.

"It seems you'd make a good teacher," said the man behind the desk a week later, after all the results had been tabulated, "particularly at the kindergarten level." He grinned, reminding Morgan of someone with a coat hanger in his mouth. "I'll bet you never thought of yourself that way, did you?"

Diane wasn't going to be home till late, so Morgan returned to an empty house and waited till 3:45, when he could pick up Alex from daycare. The daycare center was just ten minutes away during light traffic, but by 3:55 forty mothers humming along in minivans clogged the approach road, so Morgan always timed his departure accordingly. The boxy Volvo negotiated the afternoon traffic with ease as the fading sunlight squinted through the windshield. Morgan rolled down the window to get some air, letting in the autumn breeze that smelled of fallen leaves. He liked this time of day, an in-between space after house chores and before dinner, when his thoughts wandered about like errant pedestrians. For a moment, his mind was back in Diane's and his bedroom, a place of silence but little repose these days. These days it wasn't so much fatigue as insomnia. The ice-blue bedspread that Diane had brought back from a business trip to Finland somehow affected the temperature of the room. An image of Alex, his flushed face emerging from his shirt collar like some poked-up shoot, cheered him considerably. As he swung into one of the few parking spots minutes ahead of a lot of harried mothers, he smiled at his own reflection in the rearview mirror. Smile-wrinkles for Alex lined his eyes, and at age thirty-six he looked more avuncular than paternal. Eating Alex's leftovers had given him a belly and what he diagnosed as chronic indigestion.

"Afternoon, Liz," he remarked to a big woman in jeans getting out of her blue Taurus. She was here to pick up the twins, Alex and Alexis. She smiled and waved—the women were always delighted to see a male pickup.

"Hello, Mary," said Morgan softly. Mary was birdlike and always wore the same red cashmere sweater. Her daughter Aggie had recently acquired one just like it.

Then there was Rachael, with her soft dove's eyes and uncontrollable little boy Nathan. She had separated from her husband and put up with a lot of Nathan's quibbles about how Daddy would have done everything differently. At times, Nathan squirmed so much that he had to be horizontally lifted into the back seat of Rachael's old Honda.

Millie, curly-haired daughter of Sonia; Jonathan, unruly son of Pam . . . Morgan optimistically believed they were all good kids. Yet so many of the mothers looked battle weary, as if this one last chore were keeping them from ten others. And as Morgan eagerly scanned the outpouring of children from the entrance, looking for the striped polo shirt he'd dressed Alex in that morning, he dreamed up a new career.

"It's perfectly feasible," he argued with Diane that night. They were picking at the remains of a chicken potpie whose crust Morgan had burned when Alex wanted him to play catch in the backyard. "Look, a lot of these mothers would love a reliable, friendly daycare pickup service—if it were available."

"But the start-up costs, the insurance, getting to know all these parents—*and* their children," she added, dislodging a flake of pastry crust at the periphery of the burned crater. She still enjoyed his cooking, particularly since she'd finally lost the five pounds by joining a health club. "Anyway, it seems somehow . . ."

"Below me? Is that it?" Morgan leaned forward, his nose almost touching hers. "But I can't get back my old job, and I like the kids."

"Am I losing my house-husband?" she joked. At least it sounded like a joke.

Morgan snapped on a quick smile. "Think of it as regaining a wage earner."

Diane wasn't entirely wrong. The setup did take a while, with flyers to send out and advertising in the local papers, not to mention the reams of paperwork for setting up a small business. But Morgan was determined, and he went at it with the same steadfastness as in the old days when he had provided a bottle of milk at three A.M. or coaxed a stubborn appetite to eat creamed spinach. He even designed his own flowchart, which he showed to an admiring Alex. The trial route worked, and within two months he was running pickup and delivery minibuses for three daycare centers. After three months, he hired a partner, a middle-aged woman named Roz who looked like the female version of Santa Claus. Coincidentally, she was also an out-of-work teacher, downsized and divorced within the same year.

For a while, Diane seemed to like the new Morgan better, though Morgan knew he was still the same. He'd simply transferred his imagination from the classroom to the nursery and finally to the marketplace. Alex boasted of his father the bus driver until Diane took him aside and instructed him to tell people about his father the transport manager. "It means I'm trying to do a lot of different things at the same time," Morgan told him when he asked.

As Alex grew to the point where he could reply on the telephone, "Sorry, but Mommy's not here right now," Diane would call from the office, holding little conversations with him in a bright, birdlike tone. Sometimes she even took a weekend off and dragged father and son on a shopping expedition, ending at a café where Alex whined piteously for french fries.

"The problem is . . . that . . . ," she huffed to Morgan at the health club, "we're . . . drifting." Having deposited Alex at a friend's for a play date, the two of them were working out together. Diane was doing abdominal crunches while Morgan was desultorily climbing on the step machine.

He looked at her, all bent over, her face contorted in that determined pinch he knew so well. His heart softened; the beat became erratic. "You know, I still love you," he murmured. But she didn't hear him as she went on to talk about quality time. Something has to change, she told him, moving on to the leg-press. His chest ached that evening, but he ignored it. He let Alex climb all over him and rode him piggyback down the stairs.

The next few weeks were as routine as his bus schedule. Diane smiled tightly at him as she hurried out the door. Then came a series of strangely prolonged business trips, and now this disjointed phone call from Houston. Alex was at daycare, so no one else was at home, but as Diane filled up the space with what she called "discussing the issues," Morgan had to lower his voice to keep from screaming.

"I just want to say that it's nothing personal—"

"Of course not." He nodded at the receiver, at the antique clock with Roman numerals, at the gas stove on which he'd cooked so many half-eaten meals. The pain in his chest somehow lurched. At that point he must have phased out the feed from Houston because he came back in range to hear her saying something about divorce.

"What?" There seemed to be an echo in the room—he heard himself repeating that syllable a lot.

"—and naturally Alex will stay with me—I mean, I'll hire someone to look after him—"

But what Diane said after that was best known to the Houston international airport, since Morgan hung up. The kitchen had taken on a dizzy shade of mauve, the blood pounding in his temples, as he wandered about the geometric-design linoleum in an awkward circle. His first impulse was to drive immediately to the daycare center and snatch Alex away. But that would only excite comment and probably be held against him at what might turn into a court hearing. His second impulse was to call Roz and tell her to take over for the afternoon, and maybe Daddy would hit a bar or three. But that wouldn't ease all the hurt the right way. And his third impulse, to erase Diane like a stray pencil mark, was arrested by a sudden urge to lie down somewhere, anywhere, and cover his eyes.

Blundering outside the kitchen, he found himself in Alex's room, crossing the green carpet that felt like a lawn. There were the familiar toys and furniture, the game chest leering lopsidedly at him. He lay down full length in the car-bed, his head propped against the steering-wheel pillow, and wrapped one of Alex's Mickey Mouse sweatshirts about his head, shutting out the checkerboard ceiling. Mommy was far, far away. Was his whole life behind him, ahead of him, or there in that room? He held on fiercely to the sides of the bed, then more gently as his grip weakened. Who would take care of him now that he was gone, and who were "him" and "he" anyway? He took deep breaths, and things slowed down till he almost felt between heartbeats. Finally he began to see visions as if in a dream: Alex playing with his colored building blocks, Alex hiding in the closet, Alex at the wheel of the minibus, driving Daddy home, smiling in the rearview mirror.

IV

DEAR, DIRTY PARIS

ON A JUNE DAY in 1966, Andrea Empson stood at the south corner of the Gare du Nord and tried hard to look inconspicuous. On her mother's advice, she was wearing her good clothes, and now she held on grimly to the pleats of her skirt as the French girls walked by in T-shirts and jeans. The oversized hotel key, an oblong of brass and wood, stuck out of her blouse pocket because she had forgotten to return it to the clerk when leaving the hotel. She had arrived in Paris only five hours ago, somehow managed to get a room with her high-school French, and unpacked the one suitcase she had brought. It hadn't taken long.

Afterwards, she would have liked to lie down full length on the elegant four-poster bed, but at five o'clock she was supposed to meet some old friends of her parents, Mr. McGuidry and Mr. Tam. No specifics had been given, other than that they were two short gentleman who would know her on sight—"because we've written to them exactly what you look like," her mother had told her. "They're really two charming gentlemen, and they can show you around."

Andrea disliked the word *charming*; it conjured up a vision out of a Jane Austen novel, and she hoped that Messieurs McGuidry and Tam would be more like the characters in a book by Hemingway, or at least Fitzgerald. Friends of her parents tended to be on the stuffy side, like the Normans, who went to parties as lawyer and lawyer, or Mr. Michaelson, who still pinched her cheek whenever he met her, even though she was now seventeen.

Now she shifted her weight from foot to foot as she waited for the two men to come along and say hello. Two women in gauzy chemises that plunged to the navel walked by, and Andrea bit her lip. Her navy-blue skirt, white blouse, and severe leather handbag made her look like a nurse. An old man with a crooked upper lip crab-walked by, looking for cigarette butts on the station floor. He looked up at her as he passed, and his lip twisted even more in an appreciative leer. For this minuscule show of attention, she felt oddly grateful. The pallor of her legs contrasted badly with the magnificent bronze sheen of so many of the women she saw, who all seemed to be carrying a model's handbag on one arm and a boyfriend on the other.

If they don't come within the next five minutes, she decided, after the leering man had come back to her in a broad circle, I'll just go back to my hotel room. I'll telephone them I couldn't make it—no, what's their number? She could check—there probably weren't too many McGuidrys in Paris. She was just wondering why there were a McGuidry and Tam in Paris at all when someone tapped her on the shoulder. She whirled around, thinking it was the man with the leer, but it turned out to be a stump-legged gentleman in a button-down shirt and slacks. Slightly behind him was another man in an Irish green vest and fawn trousers. Something was wrong with his back because he leaned forward at an odd angle, as though an invisible hand were pushing him from behind.

The man who had tapped her on the shoulder smiled under a salt-and-pepper mustache. "Hello. Daniel McGuidry. You must be Andrea—I hope. Unless I've made a bloomer."

She looked down at him. He couldn't have been over five feet, and neither could Mr. Tam. The tip of Mr. McGuidry's nose just reached to the bra line of her blouse, making her feel a bit like an Amazon. "Yes—I mean no, there's no mistake. I'm Andrea." She nodded to the other man, who was extracting a pipe from his side pocket. "And you must be Mr. Tam."

Mr. Tam bowed deeply from the waist—there *was* something wrong with his back—and came forward to take her hand. She was so surprised when he kissed it instead of shaking it that she couldn't think of anything to say or do. Mr. Tam might have been a goatish version of Toulouse-Lautrec. The two men were so un-like her conception of her parents' friends that she wondered, just for a moment, if maybe there weren't another Tam and McGuidry somewhere in the station, and she was the wrong Andrea.

She decided to curtsy, which she did awkwardly. "I'm pleased to meet you. My parents said they knew you from years back, when they came here in . . . 1948, I think." The year before she was born.

Mr. McGuidry nodded. "Yes, '48 it was. Your mother liked making tours of the bars along Saint Michele, as I recall. Quite an outgoing spirit when she had the right amount of gin in her." His smiled broadened in recollection.

"Really?" Usually, her mother was the soul of moderation, but she did tend to drink too much at parties. Years ago, Andrea had once stayed up past her bedtime at a party her parents were giving. When she finally went to bed, she found her mother laid out full length on her coverlet, snoring gently. So that night she had slept with her father, who had asked her not to refer to the whole incident.

She pulled herself back to the matter at hand. "Anyway, it was very nice of you to agree to meet me. I don't know what you had in mind exactly. . . ." She ended the sentence with a laugh at her own expense. "I have no idea what I'm supposed to see, but I don't really want to go where all the tourists are."

"Of course, we'll be glad to show you around." Mr. Tam fitted his pipe between his teeth and struck a wooden kitchen match on the seat of his leprechaun pants. After he got the pipe drawing well, he spoke again. "What kind of things d'ya like to see?"

"I'm . . . not really sure, exactly. I've never been abroad. Whatever you think is appropriate, I guess." *Appropriate*, now there was a stupid word. They'd probably take her to the Parisian version of Howard Johnson's and order her french fries.

But Mr. McGuidry just smiled more broadly under his mustache and took her hand, fitting his rough palm against hers. "We'll find something appropriate, I'm sure. Come on, then, let's go." As if he were a small, bushy machine, he propelled both of them in the direction of the south exit, with Mr. Tam chuffing closely behind.

Where were they taking her—should she even ask? No, it was more of an adventure this way, and she was dressed well enough, in case they went to a fancy restaurant later in the evening. She did wish, though, as the hotel key jangled in her breast pocket, that she had had time to drop off the key before going out. It didn't just make for discomfort; it was a ridiculously large token, proclaiming her a tourist.

"Here, why don't you let me take that." Mr. Tam reached out and took the key, extracting it with the nimble fingers of a pickpocket. He barely brushed against her breast. "Silly thing, a key like this." He examined the embossed name. "Be better off in a different hotel, too. Why'd you go to this one?"

"My, um, my parents recommended it." With a warning about certain other kinds of hotels, she thought. Her mother was always giving her specific advice about dangers left unspecified. Her father would usually just shrug. Privately, she agreed with Mr. Tam. The clerk at the front desk wore green livery and spoke good, if accented, English, but she had wanted an old concierge with an eyeshade.

"Mm. Been a long time since your parents were here." Mr. Mc-Guidry pursed his lips, and for the first time Andrea noticed that they were purple. Against his white, stubbly face, his mouth stood out like a strip of raw meat. Maybe that's why he grew a mustache, she thought, and shifted her gaze to Mr. Tam. Both of them looked to be in their mid-fifties or older, two squat men with thick, hairy arms. They had short legs but had no trouble matching her stride. Rather, they seemed to hurry her along the sidewalk as if they were late for a show.

They passed the Place Pigalle right by; for that, Andrea was grateful. It was getting toward dinnertime, but a cloud of tourists still hung about with their cameras and children, the one around their necks and the other by their sides, with sometimes the positions reversed. The three of them, Messieurs McGuidry and Tam flanking her like two escorts alongside a battleship, passed a postcard stand, two elegant boutiques, and a bookstore where Andrea would at least have browsed if she had been alone. But they kept the same pace, taking a right at the next intersection, then a gradual left at a slanting street a hundred yards further on. She had left her map back at the hotel, but she felt that it would have been useless in any case. To use a map properly, one must first have an idea of where one is, and her sense of direction had deserted her after passing Rue Lafayette.

After entering and exiting a park so quickly that all she saw was a rush of trees, the two gentlemen slowed down a bit, which meant that she could look around. Mr. McGuidry still held her hand, and while Mr. Tam let her other hand alone, both of them pressed so close to her skirt that she could feel thigh against thigh, and they walked in synchronization, of necessity.

"Um, how did you meet my parents?" Mr. Tam was knocking

out his pipe on the park railing as Mr. McGuidry appraised the next block, possibly for a convenient restaurant. It was still a bit early for dinner, but she was eager to try authentic French food. It needn't be anything fancy, just a *croque monsieur* or an *omelette aux fines herbes*.

"Your father," said Mr. McGuidry distantly, as if he were musing on a dead man, "met us by accident. Your mother came later."

Andrea prompted him. "What was she like?" In the back of her mind was a photo of her mother from a costume ball some twenty years ago. She was dressed up as a countess, with white lace in her hair and a lorgnette hanging from a gold chain. Since her mother had always resembled a countess to her, the costume made perfect sense.

Receiving no reply to her question, she repeated it. Mr. McGuidry seemed to take it the wrong way. "She didn't dance on tables, if that's what you mean." He didn't pursue the subject, and somehow the way he looked at her made her drop it. Compared to the present, it suddenly didn't seem to matter much.

Mr. Tam broke the silence. "We were going to take you to the Tuileries, but it's too late for that now. Hungry?"

"Well, I—yes, actually. What did you have in mind?"

Mr. Tam waved his free hand. "Oh, around. There's a good fish restaurant farther on down a bit. D'ya like fish, then?"

"Oh, yes—I mean, if it's properly cooked. But I can't eat shellfish. It, um, makes me break out." She flushed, but better to come out with it now than to emerge from the restaurant looking like a gooseberry bush.

He stroked his chin. "Pity. Raw oysters are in season now. You know what *they're* good for."

The only thing Andrea knew they were good for, she had heard from a neighbor's boyfriend and chosen to disbelieve. She gave a vague nod.

Mr. Tam exchanged a glance with Mr. McGuidry. "Shall we go, then?"

"To the restaurant?" It seemed as if she had just said something stupid. Mr. McGuidry gave her hand a light squeeze. Mr. Tam nudged her from behind, and their odd procession moved forward.

The restaurant turned out to be a good deal farther down the road than Mr. McGuidry remembered. "The chef who used to run the place committed suicide when Michelin took away his star. D'ya know about the *Guide Michelin*?" He gave her hand another squeeze. Whenever she tried to tug away gently, he tugged back with the same pressure.

"Um. My mother gave me her old copy." She hadn't looked at it. "Do you mean he really killed himself, just because of what a guidebook said?"

Mr. Tam tapped his head. "Loco."

"*Non compos mentis*," announced Mr. McGuidry as they arrived at the restaurant, with a glassed-in terrace that had diners inside like goldfish. The interior looked elegant, a bit like a café scene by Degas. Inside, though, the walls were dingy. The one waiter prowling around went from one table to the next, flicking a folded napkin over the tablecloths. Most of the tables were empty. Andrea would have preferred to sit on the terrace, but Mr. Tam guided her from behind. When she veered toward the right, he nudged her with his knee.

"Ah, sorry. Thought you were going right. Waiter's at our table now."

The waiter brushed a few crumbs off the red tablecloth with the same disdainful swipe of his napkin, and moved on. After the three of them sat down—would they always be on either side of her?—he returned with glasses and tableware. He gave them each large red menus, backed with something that felt like greasy cloth.

Mr. McGuidry reached out to snap her menu shut. "Don't

bother to read the thing. We know what's good here." He winked at Mr. Tam.

Andrea frowned at her napkin. Who were these old men, anyway? They seemed to alternate between acting as her parents and something else entirely. Mr. McGuidry had the three menus piled to the left of him, and when the waiter returned, he ordered in such rapid French that she couldn't understand a word he said. "D'ya speak French?" he asked cheerfully, after the waiter had glided off.

"No, not well."

"That's good."

Mr. Tam smiled, his lips slightly apart. "Just a joke of his. We're starting with onion soup."

But when the waiter brought the soup, it was like no gratiné she had ever tasted. The gruyère cheese, if it was gruyère, had a sharp tang to it, and the onions tasted as if they had been dumped in raw.

"Like it?" Mr. Tam had already finished his bowl and now dried his upper lip on a red napkin.

She decided to be tactful. "It's not at all like what they serve in America."

"Wait till you taste the pâté." Which she took as more of a warning than a recommendation. It was gummy. The *steak au poivre* was also bad. In fact, all the food seemed to be laced with something that tasted like fennel. She ate what she could, though the only satisfactory part of the meal was the chocolate mousse, which tasted strictly of chocolate. Mr. McGuidry and Mr. Tam looked on with approval as she finished her dessert.

"No cabaret until you finish your dinner." Mr. McGuidry made a watch-checking gesture, though he had no watch. Instead, on his wrist was a pale band of skin outlining a thin red scar.

"What happened—to your watch, I mean?"

"Stolen." He signaled to the waiter for the check, leaving her to wonder if they would ever answer even one of her questions fully. They had a way of heading off all inquiries.

Out on the street again, Mr. Tam linked arms with her as casually as striking a match, and Mr. McGuidry led the way. It was getting dark outside, and if Andrea had had any idea of where she was before, she was totally lost now. Though they had started at the Gare du Nord, they had taken a lot of turns and side streets. Mr. McGuidry seemed to be heading in one consistent direction, but it was hard to tell. Every once in a while, he stopped for a moment, as if to consult some internal map. "D'ya like dancing? Or bars?"

Andrea had been thinking of a café scene more along the lines of Aux Deux Magots, though of course that was too conventional. "I don't dance much. I do drink, a little." She came out with a small, forced laugh, not echoed by the men. She tried to slow down a bit and was surprised how forcefully Mr. Tam carried her along. "Listen, why don't we go to a café for a *demi-tasse* or something? That's really all I want. And I've never been to a real Parisian café, anyway."

Mr. McGuidry considered the point as they moved along, down a street where the sidewalk was all in cracks, past a street sign that someone had bent so that the arrow pointed downward. "A café. You want to go to a café?" He exchanged looks with Mr. Tam, as if she were ten again and they were considering whether to let her stay up late that night. He patted his mustache, which every once in a while seemed to curl up of itself. It would probably be disgusting to kiss.

"How about le Gentilhomme?"

"Too far from here."

Mr. Tam disengaged his arm from hers. "No, it's not. We'll take the metro."

"All right." Mr. McGuidry turned to her suddenly, letting his hand rest on her shoulder. "You don't have a curfew or anything, do you?"

The hand was hairy right up to the second knuckle. Somewhere she had read that people with hair on their knuckles, or was it only on the first knuckle—? "No, I don't want to go to bed too early, if that's what you mean." She could bear the time lag. If she could convince these men that she wasn't a child, maybe they'd stop treating her like one. It was a tactic that often worked with her father. She reached up and took his hand off her shoulder, but in a friendly way. "We'll walk together."

"As y'please." But Mr. McGuidry kept looking over his shoulder as he walked in front of her to the metro station, and Mr. Tam, as always, insisted on bringing up the rear.

They paid for her fare—they insisted, as they had at the restaurant—which was lucky, since she hadn't had time to exchange any currency, and all she had in her purse were two twenty-dollar bills and fifteen francs a friend had given her to buy a pack of postcards. Still, she felt slightly helpless as she was herded into the half-empty subway car. Everyone on the train seemed to be in conversation with the adjacent person, except for a one-legged man with a medal on his black coat, his chin sunken into a fold of the coat. She tried looking outside, but all the stops looked similar to her, and they got off at a place that looked just like where they had gotten on. They walked up a lot of steps and were out on the street again. There was a sign that read "Blvd. Pereire," but the name meant nothing to her.

Mr. Tam looked at the intersection for a moment, then decisively turned right. The block they were now walking up had a number of sidewalk tables, with couples drinking from petite glasses and possibly discussing politics. Andrea would have stopped at any one of them, but Mr. McGuidry shook his head. He reached out to stroke her hair, a little too roughly. "Those aren't suitable. Too many *tourists*." He pronounced the word as if it had three or four syllables, and she was forced to smile.

They walked on. After the first few streets of cafés, the places began looking seedier: an awning ripped by the wind, chairs and tables with the paint coming off in large, uneven flakes. At one table in an almost-deserted restaurant, a man and a woman were shouting at each other, the man holding his fork as if he were about to plunge it into the woman's heart. There was an amused laugh from nearby, but Andrea couldn't tell in the dark whether it was Mr. McGuidry or Mr. Tam.

They passed two places that looked closed, and Andrea was just about to say that she was tired when Mr. McGuidry gently turned her rightward by the waist and said, "We're here."

The café, or whatever it was, did not look promising. There were no sidewalk tables, and a dim amber light shone through the curtains. As Mr. McGuidry steered her through the entrance— those large, strong hands—she caught a wink from the hat-check girl, who was wearing mascara that made peacock's tails of her eyelashes. Andrea smiled back, dully, wishing she had had the forethought to bring her lipstick with her.

They were led to a table by a man in a tuxedo who had teeth white as paint, and when he had safely deposited them at a table for three, he snapped his fingers for a waiter.

"What will you drink?" Mr. McGuidry cocked an eyebrow at her—shaggy, like all his hair. When he was seated, the difference in their heights balanced out, since both he and Mr. Tam had elongated torsos. From the throat of his open shirt, Mr. Tam's chest hair grew out like some black flower.

"I'll have—whatever you're having, I guess." That was stupid, she knew, but she hadn't had time to think properly. And rum and Coke sounded childish. Again, Mr. McGuidry talked in French too rapidly for her to comprehend. All she could make out was *toute* and *folle*.

Mr. Tam heaved a sigh and relaxed in his seat, though his concave back never fully touched the slats. He drummed his fingers on the tabletop as if waiting for something to happen. And in a moment, something did.

Toward the rear of the café, which Andrea now realized was the front, a purple satin curtain opened as if pulled by a delicate, feminine hand. A little stage appeared, an oval of light playing about the center. And then someone stepped into that oval of light. She was dressed in a chartreuse costume that looked as if it had been sprayed onto her. The upper half of her breasts were scooped upward from a tight-fitting bodice, which flared over her hips and more or less disappeared at the beginning of her thighs. They were wide thighs, with a shadow of muscle underneath the flesh. She smiled at the audience, looking to see who was there tonight—and she caught sight of Andrea. Her smile widened into a ruby-and-white cave.

Andrea reached for her drink, which the waiter had slipped by her elbow before gliding away. Neither Mr. Tam nor Mr. McGuidry said a word; they had their eyes on the performance. The woman onstage was beginning to undulate her hips, while her belly flexed in and out in a sinuous rhythm. A drummer just offstage began a light roll on a snare drum.

Leaving was out of the question, even if she had wanted to. There was something awful and beguiling about the woman's movements, and instead of running away, Andrea kept her eyes onstage, lifting the drink to her lips. Whatever was in the drink tasted strongly of brandy and something like apples, but harsh and medicinal. Mr. Tam was still watching the show, but Mr. McGuidry, she realized, was watching her out of the corner of his eye. She had another sip of her drink.

Meanwhile, the woman onstage was complicating her act. As her hips swung outward and her belly churned, her breasts began to heave. She reached behind her back to undo a strap, and part of her costume came free. Her breasts, now protected only by two chartreuse strips, did slow circles. Andrea felt Mr. McGuidry's garlic breath on her, but she didn't move.

The oval of light moved forward, and the dancer moved to stay with it. It floated down the steps of an aisle that passed every table. The other customers were either mesmerized like Andrea or else sucking in breath between clenched teeth, like Mr. Tam. It was obvious she was going to do a tour of the tables. Mechanically, Andrea took another sip of her drink.

The dancer advanced. Now she brushed past a man in a lizard-green suit; now she let her hand glide across a table where two businessmen were sitting. She lingered in front of an old gentleman with octagonal glasses, swinging her breasts so slowly it seemed a miracle of gravity that they moved at all. The old man hung out his tongue, and someone, maybe Mr. McGuidry, laughed. "Poor bugger."

Andrea tilted her glass, but it was empty. She put it down and the waiter snatched it, replacing it with another glass. She sipped and watched, unsure whether she was dazzled or frightened.

There seemed to be no pattern to the dancer's meandering, other than to visit each of the tables. Every once in a while, when the oval of light came particularly close to the table, Andrea could see the woman's eyes, which lit up in her direction, and her lips, which were ruby satin. It was clear she was saving this table for last.

There was no perceptible pause as she neared Andrea from the left. One of her hip-swings took her in that direction, and she followed that movement with another, and another. The oval of light omnisciently preceded her, finally coming to rest at the edge of the table. Andrea's drink was bathed in a pearly phosphorescence. She looked toward the woman, now a flesh-creature in splotches of green, and tried to draw back. She clenched her fist and found herself holding Mr. McGuidry's hand. The dancer came closer, swinging her breasts right in front of the table.

And closer: the milky white breasts, tipped with slick tan nipples, hovered in front of her, lazily rising and falling. One gently nudged her brow, and she dropped back as if she had been brushed by a live wire. The red mouth opened wide in delighted laughter, but only blackness issued forth, and the next thing Andrea knew, the woman was making her way back to the stage.

She must have passed out for a moment; she felt her arms being held as Mr. Tam chafed her wrists. She didn't like the way he was looking at her.

Mr. McGuidry checked his left wrist, but of course there was no watch. He smiled a tight smile. "I'm sorry, should we go now?" Andrea nodded, feeling moisture on her face. The dancer was ending her act, swaying toward an exit on the left. Suddenly, Andrea wanted very much to be away from this place. She got up from the table and felt the room subtly tilt. Mr. McGuidry was there to steady her.

"Easy does it. Right foot forward." He guided her out, half-holding her, while Mr. Tam followed alongside, telling her everything was fine. The hat-check girl winked at her as she was led out, and though she hadn't the strength to wink back, Mr. McGuidry winked for her. "Too much to drink," he said in recognizable French, and the hat-check girl laughed.

No, that's not it at all, it was that woman in there, Andrea wanted to say, but she didn't have proper control of her tongue, and all she could do was smile lovingly at Mr. Tam, who was helping to steer her by the waist. They turned right after leaving the café and walked a lot of blocks. The night air was getting breezy and chill, and every once in a while, she made the men stop so she could pull down her skirt, which flapped about her thighs.

"There there," said Mr. Tam, running his hand down the pleats of her skirt, smoothing the ruffles. "Don't you worry about a thing. We're going home."

The word *home* sounded strange and funny at the same time, and she giggled. Mr. McGuidry said, *"That's* a good girl," and petted her hair.

"I'm sorry, I—I've never felt this way before. Please excuse me." She was regaining control of her thoughts, though a certain fuzziness remained. She couldn't say anything about the incident in the café. That part of the night was blocked out.

"S'all right. You're just a bit dizzy, is all. You need a cup of black coffee and maybe a bed for the night. We'll take you to our place."

"Oh, no. . . ." Her voice sounded vague and distant, as if she were listening to herself on the telephone. "I don't want to bother you, have to get back anyway. They—they're expecting me," she said idiotically.

"Who's expecting you? The hotel clerk? Not likely. No, we'll take you home. You'll be much better off there." They kept walking, walking, walking. Down a narrow street with trashcans in a huddle and rusted grillwork gates. A gray cat, its huge eyes amber, pawed at one of the trashcans.

"No, you can't possibly go back to your hotel at this hour. It's too far at night." Mr. Tam's voice echoed agreeably with Mr. McGuidry's, who told her the same thing. They were like a team, or a pair of something. But she couldn't think what.

They veered off at an intersection with a horizontal traffic light, and Mr. Tam stole his hand away from her waist, leaving her unsupported. "Here we are. Two flights up."

The building was a huge gray milk carton. A bit nearer, it showed a balconied façade with three stone steps at the entrance.

It looked more decrepit than old. Andrea gripped the iron railing as she placed her foot on the first step.

"Ups-a-daisy." Mr. McGuidry nudged her from behind as Mr. Tam took her huge hotel key from his pocket, then his own keys, which he poked and twisted into the iron lock. The door swung open onto a pile of mail on the floor, which neither man looked at. They made their way up the stairs in relative silence.

"An Arab with three wives lives on the first floor," Mr. Tam mentioned as they passed the first landing. Andrea bobbed her head. Her dizziness was fading, leaving her with the same unease from before. Mr. McGuidry's arms were so hairy.

"Come in." Mr. Tam, master of the keys, unlocked the door to their apartment and stretched his hand across the threshold. Andrea walked inside.

It was only one room, as far as she could see, and it was an absolute mess. Brown-rimmed cups and dishes with egg crust were piled by the sink, and the small kitchen alcove looked as if someone had scattered lint over all the surfaces. The table still held the remnants of a breakfast, with a breadknife and a copy of *Le Jour* that reminded her of a painting by Braque. A large unmade bed stood on white metal feet over by the window. On the bedside table were a badly dented clock, a few magazines, and a pile of loose change. A notepad flanking the coins had an arrow sketched in heavy black pencil.

"There wasn't time to clean today." Mr. Tam pursed his lips. "Here, why don't you sit down, and we'll make you a cup of coffee."

"Where?" It looked as if the one chair had been kicked under the breakfast table. The bookshelf in the corner, wrought iron and cinderblock, didn't look strong enough to perch on.

"Oh, on the bed, of course. We do all our entertaining there."

He turned to Mr. McGuidry. "Do we have any of those pastries left from last night?"

"Maybe in the fridge. Please do sit down, Andrea." Mr. Mc-Guidry walked over to the bed and pulled up the covers for her. "Make yourself comfortable."

"Thank you." She sat down, keeping her eyes on Mr. Tam, who was busy at the stove with an espresso pot. What were they thinking of?—she couldn't possibly spend a night here, but what could she say? Oddly, through a trick of shadow, it looked as if the door had disappeared.

Mr. McGuidry took her hand reassuringly. His own hand was sweaty, moist. "Maybe you still feel a bit faint. If you want to lie down for a while. . . ."

She shook her head. "Maybe I shouldn't stay here, you know. It must be—it must be awfully cramped." She bit her lip; she knew it was the wrong thing to say.

Mr. McGuidry patted the bed firmly. "Nonsense, there's plenty of room. People can sleep anywhere." From the stove soon came the hissing of the coffee pot. Mr. Tam cleared the breakfast table by shoving everything onto a wooden tray, which he brought over to the sink. He returned to set three diminutive cups in a circle.

"Well, maybe I should drink the coffee and then go. I really shouldn't—"

"Of course you should." Mr. Tam was quite firm. He poured the espresso, adding little amounts to each cup until they were all at the halfway mark. "Come have some coffee, and then you'll feel better."

"I feel fine." But she didn't. The stuffy air in the room was giving her the same paralyzed feeling she had experienced in the café. She thought of getting up to take a deep breath, but the yielding surface of the mattress presented nothing to push against. It suddenly struck her that there was only one bed in the apartment.

"I really better go." She found her legs, got up a bit unsteadily, and walked toward the door. "Really, it was awfully nice of you, taking me out to dinner, and—and everything."

The door was locked. Mr. McGuidry didn't even get up from the table. "Please sit down, Andrea, and have some coffee. As a favor to us."

"All right. Okay." She didn't want to make a scene. But she would have to make them let her go; this was simply getting out of hand. She looked at the bed where they expected her to sleep the night, noticing its obscenely squashed appearance. She imagined two hairy bodies at opposite corners of it, or perhaps entwined, and felt a tremor up her thighs. Crossing over to the breakfast table, she sat down carefully in the one chair that Mr. Tam had righted for her. Her knees showed pink below the hem of her skirt. She crossed her legs.

Mr. McGuidry, meanwhile, had found the pastries he was looking for. He shoved a greasy pie plate toward her, on which were a meringue, an éclair, and an apple tart. "Here, take your pick."

"No, thanks. I had too much to eat at dinner." In fact, she was now quite hungry, but she didn't like the look of any of the pastries. Her mother would have said they were unsuitable, and for once she might have agreed with her.

"Please."

Her stomach rumbled ominously. "Well, maybe half of one." She took the biggest, the apple tart, and split it down the middle with her fingers. Then she licked each finger clean like a cat, as the two men watched her. She flushed when she realized she had been giving a performance.

"You're quite pretty when you do that."

"What?"

"That." Mr. McGuidry licked his fingers in a parody of what

she had done. "Womanly, I mean." And he reached for the other half of the tart.

"Oh." She took a sip of her espresso, strong and bitter after the taste of the pastry. "This is very good coffee," she commented, for lack of anything better to say.

Mr. McGuidry made a knot of his hands. "Strong, you mean. It's good that way. Keeps you up."

"Really? It's putting me to sleep." Maybe she would stay the night, but then she would have to leave early in the morning. She didn't want to stay around much longer than she had to. It was something about the way they looked at her, as if she weren't capable of making her own judgments. Those hairy hands . . . and now Mr. Tam was putting his arm around her shoulders. She shrank back, but against Mr. McGuidry's chest. It was strangely warm, like the furry chest of an animal.

"There there, you're getting sleepy, aren't you? Well, the bed's all ready." Mr. McGuidry's hand gently massaged her shoulder, and she was about to tell him to stop when his other hand began to knead her other shoulder. "Just relax."

"Listen, maybe you shouldn't—"

"Shouldn't what?" He dropped his hand below her shoulder blades, feeling for the sensitive area near the small of the back. Then, right then, she should have protested, and loudly, but her voice was lost somewhere near her handbag, over on the bed, or by the side of the bookshelf. Instead of saying anything, she reached out for her cup of coffee. It had a gold fleur-de-lis pattern on the outer rim.

Mr. Tam was staring at a point on the far wall, as if nothing much were happening. Mr. McGuidry was kneeling down beside her to get at the small of her back as he continued the thread of the earlier conversation. "Actually, it's a fallacy to think that good espresso keeps you up, or puts you to sleep. In dear, dirty Paris, anything can have those effects. Joyce, you know. And it *is* June 16."

"Mmm?" She felt feline, curving her spine to accommodate Mr. McGuidry's gnarled fist. She knew, too, that if she didn't get away soon, somehow, it would be too late. Too late for a number of things.

She looked at Mr. Tam, but he was no longer smiling; he simply looked interested. And Mr. McGuidry was working around to her chest. "Listen, I don't want—"

"Of course you want. All women want." With an abrupt movement of his hands, Mr. McGuidry dug into her back, forcing her chest forward, her breasts pushing against her blouse.

"Stop it, you're hurting me!" How many times had she heard that line from a movie? She kicked outward with her heel against the table, knocking over the espresso pot. Steaming black liquid splashed onto Mr. Tam, who quickly stood up to save himself. From her position, he looked tall, his face made almost handsome by anger.

"You're acting like a child, Andrea. That coffee was scalding. Say you're sorry."

"I'm—I'm sorry." It wasn't what she had intended to say. But she was sorry, sorry for Mr. McGuidry and Mr. Tam luring her here, sorry for the restaurant and the café and the apartment, most of all sorry for herself. "I'm sorry," she repeated. "I didn't mean it, at all."

Mr. Tam patted her back, incidentally sliding one hand around the back of her skirt. "Of course you didn't. S'all right, you know." Her skirt was somehow loosened and hiked up to mid-thigh. In a moment, he took hold of one leg and began to stroke it. "It's difficult, one's first night in a strange city. One doesn't know quite where to go."

"No." The coffee really had made her tired, and now, as she tried to rise, Mr. Tam rose with her, helping her under the armpits.

"*That's* a girl, mustn't slip now. Come over to the bed and lie down." Mr. McGuidry followed, coffee cup in hand, as he did something with his other hand. She craned her neck to see: he was opening the top button of his shirt.

Mr. Tam whispered in her ear, a thin stream of air that tickled lightly. "We're friends of your parents, after all. Always do right by you." Distractedly, as if reading the newspaper at the same time, he slipped off her shoes. He moved slowly upwards, gently imprisoning her legs under his weight. From outside the apartment, the light from a street lamp came in through the blinds, casting a slatted pattern over the dark area of the bed. Mr. Mc-Guidry had somehow dimmed the lights.

"I've never been to Paris, you know—I mean Europe, at all. I had no . . . no. . . ." She let the sentence trail off somewhere, out the window or under the bed. Mr. McGuidry bent over her now, face lit by the sodium light of the street lamp, his eyebrows a dark shaggy line. If it had been earlier in the evening, or in another location, or in someone else's life, perhaps she would have struck out at this oddly disjointed man, with a head too big for his body, or pulled back at the touch of Mr. Tam's callused hands. These things vaguely repelled her, and when Mr. Tam touched her thighs, she could feel her muscles tense involuntarily. Possibly, she could stop everything even now.

Instead, she stared upward at the ceiling to see a line running jaggedly across the plaster, like a crooked map. She lowered her gaze to include the overturned espresso pot, the tipsy chair, the half-made bed, and the two men like menials at her feet and shoulders. A painting she had seen somewhere, a scene from a film. The night air floated in through the window, carrying the faint sound of organ music from a radio. Mr. McGuidry was a breath away, his wet mouth open like a votary's, a dark opening circled in red. Feeling his urgency, she couldn't, wouldn't push him away. He seemed so much a part of the Parisian night.

THE ART OF THE INTERVIEW

MORTON FORCHET looked out his viewless window, sitting on his unmade bed that tripled as a chair and desk. Two columns of blue book examinations stretched high as a Roman ruin in the far corner of the room, the aftermath of Morton's composition classes this past semester, awaiting pedagogical attention with a red pen. Yet the apartment ceiling loomed as low as the brow of an idiot child, the paint was peeling from all four walls, and to add insult to an appallingly large sense of personal injury, Morton faced eviction by next week if the overdue rent wasn't paid.

Already the electricity had been cut off, an eventuality for which he had laid in a supply of votive candles, but the refrigerator was now a hulking tomb of decaying comestibles. Three cans of tuna fish and a box of soda crackers were piled haphazardly in a half-open cupboard that an earlier era would have called a larder, in one of the large Victorian novels that Morton had once devoured and now nibbled at and critically digested in order to inch along on his dissertation. From the cracked enamel sink below the window came a drip as sporadic as it was annoying, as if it considered whether to repeat itself after every *plosh*. The date was December 23, 1985, the day never a good time of year for Morton, whose mother had died from a freak case of peritonitis ten years ago on Christmas.

The phone rang, reminding Morton that not everything in his life had been disconnected. Perhaps it was his advisor, Dr. Nolan, whose florid complexion and addiction to waistcoats made him look positively Dickensian. Dr. Nolan had sparred genially with him for three years and gamely pushed him for another year before grimly settling down to the protracted argument that now substituted for academic supervision. Morton reached out for the phone receiver and paused, his arm like a bridge under completion. Maybe it was Sharon, his ex-ex-ex-girlfriend, who had broken up with him and patched things together more times than either cared to count. She was currently on the outs with him again, over a ridiculous quarrel involving the State of the Novel in a Postmodern Universe. The phone rang again, invoking repetition as well as potential discovery, the possibility that whoever was at the other end of the line was a new voice, a fresh beginning.

The phone iterated its soft burr. Third time lucky, thought Morton. "Hello?" he asked of the receiver, trying to inject a note of confidence, or to reject the timbre of defeat from his voice.

"Yes, is this Morton Forchet?" The voice, a fussy masculine version of all the professorial echoes in Morton's brain, pronounced *Forchet* the French way, though the Forchet clan stuck steadfastly to rhyming with "poor bet."

"Speaking," said Morton, to avoid the awkward predicate nominative "This is he." Advice on how to pronounce the surname could come later.

"Mr. Forchet, this is Professor Watson from Iphigenia College. We've just sorted through the applications for our job search, and we'd like to interview you at the MLA convention."

"Oh! Well." Morton had been praying for this eventuality since October, if not from Iphigenia then from one of the other fifty schools he had applied to. Unfortunately, having heard no news from anywhere by mid-December, he had accepted the inevitable, a holiday season *chez* Forchet, shared with his dour father in Missouri, for which he had already bought a bus ticket. He certainly couldn't afford to head for California on the off chance that he might catch someone's eye, and he had almost smugly resigned himself to missing the convention. That was all right—he'd attended last December's caucus in Chicago and found enough alienation to last him all year. The fact that most schools did all their hiring at these conventions, when he didn't seem even potentially salable, hadn't helped. One of these days, something will turn up, he'd thought, unconsciously mimicking Mr. Micawber.

And now this. There was a long pause, punctuated by the reliably unreliable faucet drip.

"Mr. Forchet? Are you still there?"

"*Yes!* I mean, yes. And I'm delighted that you're interested in an interview," he went on, sliding into a practiced tone as smooth as furniture polish. "Actually," he continued rather lamely, "I don't think I'll be attending the convention this year."

It was the phone receiver's turn to pause. "Hmm," pontificated the voice. "It looks like you're located in New Jersey. This is slightly irregular, but I suppose if you're willing to come to campus, we could interview you there, after the convention."

A clarion reprieve! A vote of confidence when his self-esteem hung as low as the red-tinted mercury in the outdoor thermometer (with a current reading of below freezing). At the moment, Morton couldn't exactly recall where Iphigenia was, his mind preoccupied with images of gainful employment and brightly shining students who called him "Professor Morton." Sure, he'd get to Iphigenia wherever and whenever, and he was going to snag that job. How could he fail now? He smiled experimentally, but the nearest mirror was in the cesspit of a bathroom, so he couldn't properly gauge its effect.

"Certainly, Professor Watkins—"

"Watson."

"Sorry, must be a bad connection. Yes, Professor Watson, I'll be there with bells on! So to speak." He bit his underlip. Mustn't seem overeager—they'll think you're desperate. But you are desperate, insisted a voice from his parietal lobe, which he suppressed.

"Good. Let's just set up a time then. Shall we say January 2, three o'clock? 321 Palmer Hall. And do you need directions to get here?"

"Oh, no, no. No, that'll be all right." Show your competence from the start. "I've got maps," he explained.

"Well, okay. But the bridge from Allston is sometimes out of commission this time of year, in which case you have to take a detour on 571."

"Fine, I'll trace out a route," he insisted. Now where the hell had he put those maps?

"Then we look forward to seeing you on the second. Bye now." The voice from the other end segued into a click and a dial tone.

Morton waited a careful moment before springing from his bed-chair-desk and capering about on the threadbare carpet. An end to this miserable graduate-student existence and the slave labor of teaching composition classes to the educationally challenged! Of course, Iphigenia hadn't agreed to hire him yet, but that was a detail. While the other interviewees would be strutting their stuff within the cramped confines of a hotel room in San Diego, he would be on the campus itself, already on-site, a *fait accompli*.

But first: location. A spirited half-hour search revealed that his Rand McNally atlas was propping up the front left leg of his stove. Reaching under the desk portion of his bed-chair, he rummaged around for his application letters. Furman, Goucher, Howard. . . . There it was, slightly obscured by a dust mouse the size of a rabbit. "Dear Dr. Watford"—damn, why couldn't the man stick to one name?—"I wish to apply for the position of assistant professor in 19th-century British literature." He checked the address and consulted the atlas, whose dog-eared pages had been rendered translucent by something like salad oil. Iphigenia was in a town of the same name in upstate Vermont close to the Canadian border, a dot the breadth of a period linked to no major or even minor roads.

He called up the toll-free bus and train information services, but nothing came close to Iphigenia. Nothing even neared Allston, the next-biggest dot on the map. He'd have to rent or borrow a car, though the only car owner with whom he was on anything approaching friendly terms was Sharon, and she wasn't speaking to him. These intervals, or extervals as he mentally tabbed them, had been known to last as long as a semester or as short as a sentence.

He had a sudden image of her in that pilling blue sweater he knew a little too intimately, nervously raveling a sleeve as she frowned over an edition of Roland Barthes and highlighted a salient passage. She had a good mind and a not-bad body but, like most graduate students, hid them under layers of clothes and intellectual truculence. His mind wandered from her pointy breasts to the sexy chassis of her little Fiat Uno, which was still running, as far as he knew, though the gas gauge had a Pollyanna-ish way of reading FULL until the tank was suddenly empty, and the engine block leaked a strange viscous fluid that no auto mechanic had quite been able to identify.

Telephone her now, don't call, of course call, better not try it—but you have to, he concluded after staring out his viewless window for almost a minute. The vista resembled his situation insofar as it offered no options, just a brick wall with a pale wedge of sky from one awkward angle. He dialed her number and waited three, then four rings. If the short phone cord had allowed him to pace, he would have. Instead he had to content himself with a little hip-swivel on the bed.

A "hello" with all the warmth of a wake greeted him on the seventh ring.

Knowing he had to get past her defenses before she hung up on him, he spewed out his message: "Listen Sharon it's me Morton and I'm sorry to bother you but we really need to talk so I figured I'd just call up and hey I'm sure glad you're home."

A pause hung in the air like a balloon of uncertain hue. Finally Sharon blurted out, "Oh, Morton, it's so sad around here! Argyle died yesterday." Argyle was Sharon's aged alley cat, a feral-looking creature who for reasons best known to itself guarded Sharon's books and had more than once scratched Morton's face when he'd gotten too close.

"Really? That's awful," he lied. "How'd it happen?"

"It was dreadful—he was climbing up one of my bookshelves when he slipped and brought a whole shelf down. I don't think it was the novels so much—it was my Webster's Unabridged."

The term *situational irony* flitted through Morton's mind like a bat at dusk and settled in the belfry of his consciousness. He felt a neat satisfaction whenever life imitated a literary trope. A poet like John Suckling could have made a mini-epic of it: "Verses on the Death of Argyle, A Feline Crushed by the Weight of Letters." This was not a thought to communicate to Sharon, however, and turning an incipient chuckle into a throat-clearing noise, he found some suitable words of bereavement.

"Thanks, Morton, you're a mensch." Her voice calmed down, even turning tender. "I'm glad you called."

"Look, I'm sorry about—"

"That's okay." Sharon's interruption was fortuitous since he'd blanked on what he was supposed to apologize for. After a few more protestations and aposiopeses, they arranged to have dinner the next day and left it at that.

Morton hung up and clapped his spatulate hands together in anticipation. Part one of the plan was under way: after several days to worm his way back into her affections, he would subtly bring the subject around to transportation and ask to borrow her car.

He peered about his room. Already, with the promise of a job or at least a promising interview, the confines of his apartment soared, the walls a slightly cheerier shade of beige. The twin ionic columns of blue books looked almost picturesque, but in any event he had no intention of attending to them, not when he had to prepare for his interview. He had one respectable suit that badly needed pressing, a summary of his dissertation to be spun out of the air, perhaps a sample syllabus or two to produce when they asked what he could teach, a smile that required a little practice to get that anxious twitch ironed out of it—so much to do, and it occurred to him that he hadn't even eaten breakfast yet.

He was just reaching for the ever-ready box of soda crackers when he pulled himself up short. "Morton Forchet," he intoned, self-address his chosen form of sententiousness, "considering the altered circumstances, you deserve a real meal." He carried the dialogue a step further by patting himself on the back. His pale, gangling body accepted the complimentary gesture. "C'mon, let's go. I'm treating." In a moment, the warped apartment door shut with a combination creak and thud as he walked out to encounter an odor he hadn't sniffed in a while: fresh air.

After an egg-and-something platter at McCann's Diner, a favored hangout of the economically depressed, he began to feel even better. Slightly awash from his bottomless cup of coffee, he sketched out his designs on a paper napkin. Assistant professor of English at Iphigenia next fall, tenure awarded in his sixth year along with a promotion to associate status, followed by a sabbati-

cal during which—but he had run out of space on his tri-fold napkin and drained his coffee cup, and rather than start on another
cup and napkin, he paid his check and left. No birds sang in the
sidewalk trees—it was December, after all—but he felt like chirp-
ing a bit himself, and did.

That afternoon he scooted to the university library to check
out Iphigenia in the mammoth microfiche collection of college
catalogues. At first he couldn't find the listing and experienced
the kind of panic resembling the scratchy interior of a nightmare.
But there it was, misfiled in the catalogues for the alphabetically
adjoining state of Utah. How absurd that an entire school could be
summarized in a slice of acetate the dimensions of a note card, he
thought, as he slipped the fiche into the machine, read something
like "ǝƃǝlloƆ ɐᴉuǝƃᴉɥdI," and reinserted it face up.

Founded in 1924, situated near Lake Penwagon . . . he hurriedly
skipped to academics and scanned the English department roster.
The chair, Professor Glen Watson, headed up a faculty of twelve,
including someone intriguingly named Horace Mulewright. No
one he recognized there, though he scribbled down their names to
check later for possible publications. The course offerings looked
unimaginative, from "Shakespeare: Selected Plays" to "The Twen-
tieth Century: Representative Literature of This Period." He wondered how his dream course, "The Victorian Closet: Libido and
Liebeschmerz" would fare at Iphigenia, and rejected it out of hand.
There'd be time for that later, after he'd published his dissertation
and secured tenure.

Since it was two days before Christmas, he shared the entire
library with one pimply work-study undergraduate interested in
shutting off all the lights. Closing time, the student intoned sepul-
chrally, was in twenty minutes, after which the library would re-
open in January. Scooting over to the computerized humanities
indexes, Morton started frantically looking up names. Curiously,

the English department faculty of Iphigenia didn't seem to have published much of anything in the last twenty years, except for Horace Mulewright's monograph *Some Obscure Latin Epigrammatists* (Melody Press, 1982). That was all right, though: it meant that his own publication, a three-paragraph book review in *Nineteenth-Century Literature* two years ago, might be acceptable without seeming overly assertive. Feeling he had put in a good day's work, he went home and read Trollope for the rest of the afternoon. That night he augmented his supply of foodstuffs, adding sardines to his canned tuna collection and a box of tea bags to sit alongside his crusted jar of instant coffee. He went to sleep that night with a clear or only slightly streaked conscience.

The next day, after a ponderous half-hour dealing with a non-comprehending clerk, he got a refund on his bus ticket for Missouri. His father, the next person he called, accepted the news with seeming resignation and a deep instigation of guilt. "I guess you know what you're doing," he remarked doubtfully, his grizzled features intruding a grizzled note over the phone. "Maybe I'll see you one of these days."

Morton felt bad that he didn't feel worse about this, but he didn't, so he wished his father happy holidays and left it at that. The next chore was to start work on a description of his dissertation so that he could rattle it off for the interviewing committee. He spent all afternoon juggling clauses of a sentence that included Victorian novels and the politics of narrative, balanced as an off-the-cuff answer to "Can you tell us about your current research, Mr. Forchet?" and ending at dusk with a snarled "Who wants to know?" in the bathroom mirror. But he refused to be discouraged by his lack of progress, and he reinverted his snarl into a smile in preparation for his Christmas Eve dinner with Sharon.

Sharon's apartment was on the other side of town in a higher rent district. Compared to Morton's living quarters, it was smaller but nicer, like Sharon herself. When Morton arrived at seven o'clock, he saw a wreath on the door, which at first shocked him because he knew Sharon's dim view of Christmas, then more subtly appalled him when he learned that it was a mourning wreath for Argyle.

"I want him to know he's gone but not forgotten," murmured Sharon, her cat-hairy sweater still a testament to the presence of her pet. The fatal bookshelf, Morton noted, had been dismantled. Exuding what he hoped was the proper measure of sympathy, he pawed the carpet and nervously wondered what had been done with the corpse.

In any event, Sharon's grief was an on-and-off event. Sorrowful one moment, in the next instant she gave Morton a fierce kiss. "Let's have dinner in," she purred, though after five minutes of opening and shutting kitchen drawers, she cried "I miss him!" with a wail worthy of the dear departed. Dinner ended up a lachrymose affair of wilted salad and tuna-noodle casserole, which he wouldn't have minded so much if he hadn't subsisted on similar fare for the past week.

He'd intended to tell her about the interview, but the funereal atmosphere didn't encourage such an expansive confidence. Oddly it did encourage sex, consummated on the orange sofa in an awkward postprandial embrace. Scratched and hairy as it was, the sofa itself was a feline *memento mori*, as if Argyle were there in both spirit and body. In fact, as Morton groped Sharon's sweaterly breasts, he felt as if he were making love to a catwoman. As she roamed over his body with her sharp nails, he had the impression she was grooming him.

The sex itself was mutually satisfying, though they rarely generated as much friction as they did in their intellectual arguments. In bodily matters, both tended to yield too quickly, and the act was over in the space it would take to read five pages of D. H.

Lawrence. Afterwards, Sharon stretched luxuriously, one of the few luxuries she allowed herself. Morton contented himself with a contented sigh, feeling slightly inadequate. In atonement, he embarked on a provocative discussion about eros and anomie. Morton was for Sade, who preached control; Sharon was for Henry Miller and chaos. They played with the idea, batting it about like a ball of yarn for a few minutes until they reached a point where they agreed to disagree. They both held back from pushing it further, the cause of their last breakup. Morton left around eleven on Christmas Day with a promise for a New Year's date and a sleazy feeling of accomplishment. They didn't exchange gifts and felt smugly pagan about this.

*

The days between Christmas and New Year's, Morton spent in dreaming up creative ways to heat his apartment (stopping just short of incinerating his dissertation in the gas stove) and further preparing for the upcoming interview. Huddled in his overcoat, he scribbled notes for prospective courses: "Aspects of the Victorian Novel," "ABC: Austen to Brontë to Conrad," "Dickens and His Circle." Looking gloomily over at the twin stack of blue books, he added "Freshman Composition."

The third day, he thought of calling Dr. Nolan for advice, though he knew his advisor usually left for Florida this time of year. After three rings, an answering machine kicked in with the spidery rewind of an old film projector: "This . . . is Floyd Nolan. . . . I'll be away . . . in San Diego at the MLA convention . . . from December 27 to the . . . 31. If this is an emergency . . . you can reach me at the San Diego Ramada. Otherwise . . . leave a message after . . . the tone." For reasons best known to Dr. Nolan or his answering machine, no tone was forthcoming at the end, and Morton didn't have the heart to pursue the matter further.

Instead, he warmed up his arms by flapping like a chicken and practiced his handshake for a while. The polite clasp was paired with "Hello, I'm Morton Forchet. It's a pleasure to meet you." The type who looked like a bonecrusher heard "Hi. Mort Forchet. Pleased to meet ya." He also nodded expectantly and smiled. Through sheer daily practice, his rictus was growing wider.

As he thrust his hand forth repeatedly into the chilly air, his thoughts strayed to the convention in sunny San Diego, and he wished he were Dr. Nolan, paunch and all, relaxing at the Ramada. Or better still, a fly on the wall of the interview room for Iphigenia College. Ten or fifteen candidates over the course of two or three days—and what about him? Last seen, best thought, his father had told him, though he'd been talking about his dead wife.

And what of the interviewers? He retracted his hand and gazed out the window, where imaginary professorial profiles began to drift along the brick wall. The gent with old-fashioned spectacles and a yellow bow tie slightly askew, that had to be Horace Mule-wright. Glen Waters came next, tweedy and fussy, his lips compressed as from a clothespin. The one woman on the faculty—what was her name? Daphne-something—had upswept frosty hair to match her frosty expression, though Morton suspected she could be won by the right combination of charm and artifice. Others followed in shadowy profile, the massed English faculty of his destiny.

When he blinked, the whole procession twitched back into brick and mortar. He ate a solitary meal of tuna and crackers, enlivened by half a cucumber, and settled in for the night. When he tried calling Sharon later, she wasn't home—so where the hell was she? Hadn't she said something about a brief trip in between Christmas and New Year's? He'd accepted his miserable state for so long, the implication that other graduate students had a life bothered him. Of course, things would be different when he was ensconced at Iphigenia. That night, he had an absurd dream in which he received a magnificent job offer from a nude Dr. Wadley as the ragged remains of his composition classes cheered him on from the football bleachers. He woke up at ten A.M. with the coverlet around his ankles and the scurfy taste of the dream still in his mouth. In the cold gray morning, the memory of his ghostly support group propelled him guiltily in the direction of the blue books, which really should have been graded a week ago.

The final exam for English 101 was simple enough: three separate essays, one taking a stand on a social issue like abortion, one taking the opposite stance, and one on writing an essay, all to be completed within three hours. Now seated at the edge of his desk-chair-bed, the first batch of blue books scattered in front of him like 52 Pick-Up, he reached out for a random sample.

"In my opinion I think the death penalty should be universal all over especially for criminals," began one first page winningly. "If you crime yourself"—Morton peered at the new verb—"you should be crimed in return." He thought he recognized the style: Jenny Ransom perhaps, the blonde with the permanent scowl in the back row; or maybe Stan Maynard, who was so clearly a football player that the whole vexed issue of academics seemed beside the point. Sighing wearily (his students called him "Steam Engine Forchet"), he moved in with his red pen and began correcting right and left. He was halfway through his fifth blue book when he knocked over his cup of coffee onto the remaining stack and created the Brown Sea. Discouraged and taking this as a sign, he blotted his desk with more blue books, shoved the whole pile into a corner, and wisely refrained from correcting any more.

On the fifth day, or was it the sixth, he began improvising make-believe conversations with the interviewing committee. "I'm glad you asked me that," he would smile as he paced around his room. "Yes, I really do admire some of the later writings of

Nietzsche. As the excesses of a strong mind, I mean," he added as the friendly expression of Daphne Whatsername grew frosty again. He paused to straighten his posture. At other times, he tried returning to his dissertation, the relevant books and stacks of papers in the far corner of the room, but that was truly hopeless. The sequence of days was becoming slightly surreal, like a trick shuffle revealing the same card over and over again, and with a start he realized it was December 31.

My God, tonight was his date with Sharon, and he still hadn't told her about the loan of her car! In mid-afternoon, he flew about his apartment preparing and packing, since he might not have time in the next day or two. He also hadn't remembered to dry-clean his suit, and there certainly wasn't time for that now. Fingering the lapels that looked folded and spindled if not quite mutilated, he recalled a stratagem that a college roommate had taught him: hang an item of clothing on the shower curtain rack, turn on the hot water, and let steam do the rest. After an hour of this treatment, however, all Morton had to show for it was a drenched suit. It would dry, but with even less shape than before. What with one thing and five others, he made it to Sharon's apartment in a foul temper by seven o'clock.

"Come in, come in," purred Sharon, and Morton was glad at least to see that the wreath had been removed from the door. She was wearing what looked like a new green sweater with minimal pilling and no evidence of cat hairs. Her grin, which had the odd effect of looking broader than her face, temporarily defused his moodiness. She stroked his chin, which was almost successfully shaven. He nibbled at her hair, redolent of synthetic apple blossom.

"How about the Blue Elk?" suggested Morton when it came time to go out for dinner. "They've got candlelight."

"Sure." Sharon pursed her lips. "Or we could go to Lavinia's if you're in the mood for pasta."

He nodded. "Maybe. Though we might try Oscar's if you want to go downscale." They were playing the accommodation game, solicitous to the other's needs while pushing other options. They finally decided on a place called The Tavern, insofar as it was New Year's Eve. Morton's main concern was to choose a place far enough to require the use of Sharon's Fiat, and The Tavern was a good five miles away. They walked out hand in hand, and to his relief the little Fiat started up with only a brief spate of coughing. Apart from the cat-scratched passenger's seat, which provoked Sharon to a nostalgic sob, it seemed quite serviceable.

People with ulterior motives are odious, announced a small voice in his mind. Kindly shut up, he told it. Everyone has hidden motives. All right, but this damn well better work, growled a third voice that sounded more like the voice of his pragmatism than his conscience. Sharon, manipulating the gearbox of the Fiat, heard nothing.

Dinner at The Tavern made up in noise what it lacked in romance, and as the evening progressed they grew rather drunk. Their talk on Walter Pater—for their conversations were usually literary—began to meander. "I think we're slightly sloshed," pronounced Morton after Sharon knocked over her third margarita.

"Shlightly shloshed," she giggled, and they toasted their inebriation with a glass of champagne at midnight. Morton insisted on driving them home (another calculated move, to get the feel of the car), and they passed an enjoyable catless night at Sharon's apartment.

The morning after was Morton's undoing. He'd intended to broach the subject of the car loan after breakfast and a leisurely grope. Instead, he found himself arguing about postmodernism after a perhaps innocent remark of Sharon's about Beckett. How the hell had it even come up?

"What you don't know about postmodernism would fill volumes," snorted Sharon, showing her lumbar curve as she sat up in bed. "You are what you specialize in, and you're a Victorian. Everyone knows that."

"Well, at least I'm not in perpetual mourning for some damned feline! What good's a dead cat except as fertilizer?"

A few volleys followed this exchange, the last delivered to the slam of Sharon's apartment door. Only then did a numb despair begin to open inside him as if a gravedigger were digging for a plot in his lower stomach. God, what now? Yet shoving his hands into his pockets for the slow walk back, he discovered a jingly item that altered the situation considerably: Sharon's car keys from the night before. He examined the key ring, a wire loop suspiciously like a used IUD, with growing excitement. Since Sharon drove her car about once a week, she might not miss these for a while. Stealing—no, borrowing—the car, was that such a reprehensible act? His only twinge of regret, quickly suppressed, was that he didn't feel guiltier. It would have made him feel more human, somehow.

But there wasn't any remorse. In fact, he felt better and better. His defeated march home turned into a saunter, and by the time he reached his apartment he was almost skipping. Life, liberty, full employment! Not even the yellow eviction notice he found slid under his door could deter him now. Who cared about cheap rooms when he'd be able to afford professorial lodging soon? He stood in front of his brick-wall view and pronounced his future title: "Dr. Morton Forchet"—well, not until he'd finished his doctorate, but that was just a detail. "Professor Morton A. Forchet," then. The "A" was for Alphonse, not a name he particularly cared for, but the initial lent a certain gravity.

His suitcase yawned open like an alligator jaw from where he'd left it on his bed-desk, its gorge half-crammed with prep notes, a few cans of tuna fish, toiletries, a map, and his dried-out suit. Since the interview was tomorrow at four, he would make his move in the gray concealment of dawn, before Sharon was up. The rest of the day he spent pacing, occasionally rubbing his wrists together as much in anticipation as from the cold in the room, which was increasingly arctic. He rehearsed what he regarded as key sentences. "Why, I'd love a cup of coffee, Professor Waters," he murmured as he poured himself one. "I'm glad you asked me that question." He turned toward the wall. "So you're Professor Mulewright! I read something of yours a while back . . . Latin epigrams, wasn't it?" He shook hands with himself politely, energetically, and halfway between. He kicked the blue books, slowly decomposing into a sodden mass, further into the corner. Finally he turned in early, drawing back the quilt from his desk and scrabbling inside like a mole. He set his wind-up alarm clock for four A.M., blew out the last votive candle, and shut his eyes firmly.

Insomnia beset him at once, little gray men who danced on his eyelids and whispered tender threats in his ears. But the prospect of the imminent job soothed him sufficiently so that he dropped off to sleep around one A.M.—only to be wakened by the buzz saw of his alarm clock at an hour when the brick wall outside was dark as ivy, blending seamlessly into the swatch of sky above.

Half swearing, half humming, he stumbled to the bathroom to shower and shave, managing to cut himself only twice, which he counted as a good augur. Dressing hurriedly, he gulped down an improvised meal of coffee and crackers. He stuffed a last handful of papers into his suitcase, more for ballast than anything else, and banged it shut. For a moment, he stood still as a book, casting a cold eye over his past. Would he even return to this room again? The warped door shut behind him like a gate. In a moment he was on the street, hoofing it to Sharon's place.

In the dull light of predawn, everything from shadows to parked cars displayed the illusion of perpetual fixity. The Fiat was situated exactly where he'd left it two nights ago, its windshield eyeing him with the half-lidded lethargy of an animal in hibernation. Yet he could swear it perked up as he approached. He reached out stealthily to pat it, opened its trunk, and tossed his suitcase inside. Once installed in the driver's seat, he turned the ignition key and pumped the gas till he heard a satisfying rumble, and pulled away in a plume of blue-gray smoke. Three-quarters of a tank, the seat adjusted properly, the steering wheel snug in his hands— everything conspiring to get him to his appointed destiny, and it was about time, damn it. By the time he reached the freeway, the map was unfolded, the heater was working full blast, and he could already see a small school ahead of him called Iphigenia, a paneled room where he would greet the committee, the very chair where he would sit and demurely cross his legs. A very pleasant trip, thank you. I'm glad you asked me that question. He tried on his smile, grown elastic as taffy, in the rearview mirror.

Yet as he drove down the accessway ramp for Route 95, the broken arc of the future was already beginning to fall: the way the Fiat engine would begin to sputter after the first thirty minutes and finally die seven miles from an exit; the bum mechanic he would reach after several frantic phone calls, who would bring it back to his shop only to conclude that it needed a part he'd have to order specially; how his wallet would be stolen from him in the nearby diner where he'd gone to warm up, shutting off all possibility of further phone communication; the dull three hours of hitch-hiking to somewhere near Iphigenia, in the process losing his suitcase, only to find that the bridge near County Road 571 was, as he'd been warned, impossible to cross in January; that after a combination of hiking and slogging in the increasing dusk, he would arrive for his interview ten hours late, pounding on the door of Palmer Hall, calling for Dr. Watley, Wattle, Whatsisname, as the frightened security guard called for reinforcements . . . but for now, he was determined as a bull terrier, his nose quivering in anticipation as he glanced at himself in the mirror, readying himself for the interview, driving straight as an arrow up his highway of dreams.

METAFICTION

I BEGAN by telling them what I expected. They seemed an average bunch, casually grouped around the heavy wood furniture that the university leaves in the fine-arts rooms like children's building blocks. Two individuals who later turned out to be Dan and Cynthia were both perched on the blue table-cube, slanting together. Hargrove sat straight up in a chair with a ramrod back, his pen poised at a forty-five-degree angle. One of the women, Jennifer, I'm sure, sat in the only comfortable chair, a mahogany monstrosity with armrests like thighs. Kate was in the corner—of course—in a collapsible chair that she would neatly fold up at the end of every workshop. There was also one other student, who left after the first session and whose name I can't recall, though I've tried.

In some writing workshops, the instructor assigns an anthology, prescribes exercises and regular assignments, and monitors each individual's progress. In other classes, the person nominally in charge asks to see something the student has written by the end of the term. I tend to be somewhere in the middle. This applies to my teaching as well as my own writing and life, I've come to realize.

Most jobs for writers in academia gradually make one feel like a professor who writes on the side, and I had begun teaching at

Hopewell three years ago. My first and only novel, *The View from Parnassus*, had come out the year before that, and in the interim all I'd been able to spin out were a few short stories and half a draft of what by now was clearly not going to be my second novel.

Give me credit for not taking it out on my students. In fact, in overcompensation, I took extreme pains to keep my private life out of the class. My students knew me as Mark Hopkins, a clean-shaven blond man in his early thirties who walked in every Tuesday at three o'clock to teach writing. If they bothered to look up *The View from Parnassus*, they still wouldn't have known much more than that because I made up most of the details in the book. That's what imagination is for: to compensate for your life. For my part, I tried never to read too much into what my students delivered to me, whether it was a dorm room description or a dark night of the soul.

Six students in a class was skimpy even for a workshop, but it also meant less work for me. Hopewell isn't a bad school, and I'd spotted some real talent, but I'd also gotten to that unhealthy stage where less is more—less work to plow through, more time for me—even if I wasn't using that time to anyone's advantage. Lately, I'd discovered a local haunt named Capper's, and some of my best hours were spent wrapped around a scotch on the rocks. Hemingway, I'd decided, was an invention of drunk writers everywhere.

So much for setting and background. As I stood at the front of the room that first day, I had that "here we go again" feeling that only a teacher or a cast member of a long-running show can appreciate. I explained that I'd be asking them to hand in six pieces of writing during the course of the semester. Three would be assigned; three would be on their own. We would be reading excerpts from *The Norton Anthology of Short Fiction*, a bulky volume I had gotten thoroughly sick of but was too lazy to change.

Hargrove raised his hand as if trying to touch the ceiling. I had said that anyone could just speak out, but he always insisted on the formality. Even his Afro was somehow regulation. "Mr. Hopkins" (the others soon called me Mark), "where do we buy the book?"

"They sell it at the university bookstore." Kate pulled out a copy from the book bag at her feet and held it as if she'd brought it for Show & Tell. It was the kind of fat paperback that instantly cracks its spine and flops open obscenely in public places. She blushed prettily as it swung wide, baring the heart of a Katherine Mansfield story.

Dan and Cynthia looked at each other and looked away again. As if by mutual consent, Cynthia spoke. "Do you want us to, uh, keep a journal or anything?"

"If you want." I was the soul of neutrality. "But it's not required." Meaning that no one would do it.

Dan nodded for the two of them. I couldn't decide whether this was a relationship or symbiosis. Jennifer made herself ever more comfortable in her chair, leaning back and spreading her legs as if she were in a gynecologist's office. The nameless student appropriately said nothing. I don't know whether he was intimidated or just bored, but teachers always take these things too personally. Maybe he dropped the course because of a schedule conflict. Or maybe he didn't like the first assignment.

Write three pages of a dialogue between two characters evoking a third character.

This is trickier than it sounds, especially if it's done right. Ideally, what you have by the end are three separate personalities. Since it's more interesting to criticize than to praise, what I usually see is a lot of anonymous character assassination. The commonest paradigm is two women dissecting a current or ex-boyfriend. A close second is two men discussing the sexual availability of some woman.

We started off the next class with Jennifer's piece, since she was the only one who didn't mind going first. True to form, it featured two women taking apart the first woman's lover: his hair, his height, the way his feet smelled, how he normally walked, how he walked into a dark room with a naked woman on the couch, and what ensued. The viewpoint was that of two experienced females talking about an inexperienced male. The tone was amused, and the author clearly wanted to be amusing, but when I asked the class whom they sympathized with, all of them voted for the male. All except for Hargrove, who looked at his feet—I think some of the anatomical details had embarrassed him.

Coincidentally, Hargrove had also written about an evening tryst, but from the more difficult vantage of praise, with a scoffing interlocutor. Oddly, the woman sounded entrapping, the man somewhat naive. When I asked for the sympathy vote again, three voted for the man, with one opting for the woman—Jennifer, I think.

The other sketches were harder to classify and not too memorable. For a while, we discussed realism in dialogue, and what a person could or wouldn't mention in ordinary conversation. It's hard getting your own physical traits across if you're the one who's speaking, for example, but it's possible (see the description of Mark Hopkins, a clean-shaven blond man in his early thirties, in paragraph four). For the record: Jennifer had chestnut hair and a sexy, loose-limbed body; Kate was petite with mousy hair; Hargrove was tall and slender with a flat face; Dan looked like Mr. Average, down to the number of freckles on his arms; and Cynthia had the grub-white pallor that earlier generations thought aristocratic.

Occasionally, I would see them on campus: Hargrove staring

balefully at a sandwich at the student center, Kate carrying her flute case to an orchestra rehearsal, or Dan and Cynthia surgically attached at the hip as they walked to the library. Jennifer seemed to attract all of them in random groupings, so at any given time she'd be with Dan and Cynthia, or Kate, talking earnestly about whatever it is that students talk earnestly about these days. I'd say hello and move on, aware of my own distance from them. A pedagogical barrier. One night I had a dream in which Jennifer and Kate were teaching me, and I woke up in a sweat.

The third week, they were free to write what they wanted. The fallback project in case they pulled a blank was a complete character sketch that included all five senses. Naturally, they all opted for the directed assignment rather than risk something unknown.

Still, it was gutsy of Cynthia to write about Dan. At first, it wasn't clear whom she was describing: he was a boy in her calculus class with a crooked frown when he was puzzled. His voice was high-pitched and accelerated when he got going. When she brushed his arm accidentally on purpose, she was surprised to find it so smooth. It was silky in a sensual way, and he made her feel hairy. He had absolutely no odor whatsoever. When they made out on their first date, he tasted like mint because he'd been sucking a wintergreen LifeSaver.

Cynthia didn't look at Dan while she was reading, but then they usually sat back to back. It was only when she got to the part about wintergreen and I saw Dan had something in his mouth that I made the connection. I mean, would you write about your boyfriend if he were in the same class? In fact, Dan didn't look embarrassed while she was reading the sketch; more absorbed, I'd say, as if checking the details for accuracy.

We talked about which details mattered and why. I pointed out that the olfactory sense is left undeveloped in most fiction. Then Dan read his piece about Cynthia. "The first thing that hits you is a strong smell of crushed violets," he began. He also described how she smelled after sex (like the lion cage at the zoo) and after a shower (soap flakes with a hint of balsam). Cynthia bit her lip but said nothing—it was curious that Dan had given her no words, having forgotten the auditory sense. If the others knew what was going on, they kept it to themselves. The comments were noncommittal. Hargrove looked mortified, but I gathered that anything sexual would have that effect on him. He was in for a rough semester.

Kate's sketch also concerned a smooth-skinned boy, though more the Prince Charming type from an inverted fairy tale. That is, she was the one who rescued him from the clutches of another girl, a sort of tigress who had kept him on a very short leash. In fact, she spent as much time describing the other girl as she did the boy, who seemed a cipher in all of this. It's hard to describe exactly, since the original writer found it hard, but the sum of his traits added up to zero. Any life he had came from physical description: "skin the color of soap"; "almost soundless as he walked"; "a faint smell of burnt toast hung about him from breakfast." Kate's prose was simple, proper, and touching—though I wonder whether that was in her style or from what I thought of her. By the end of the course, circumstances had changed, and so had her tone.

The rest of the group handed in story drafts they were working on. Jennifer's incorporated the dialogue she had written the week before, with an added twist: the boy being talked about had rejected the first speaker, possibly in favor of abstinence, possibly in search of a male lover—it was hard to tell. But there was definitely a growing intimacy between the two women, even a hint at coupling. Sex seemed so available in these stories, or maybe it was just wish fulfillment. When I saw Jennifer sprawled in a club chair at the library one afternoon, her left foot grazing Kate's ankle, I had to repress an urge to separate them. Or join them myself.

The truth is that all this fictional bed hopping made me feel left out. A month ago I had broken up with a girlfriend with liquid eyes who smelled of Chanel No. 5, and I hadn't found a substitute yet. Hence the hours spent in Capper's, alternately searching for prospects and whining about my fate. But teaching always yanks me back from self-pity with the attraction of doing good. Next week I intended to concentrate on plot, something my own life lacked at the moment.

Use the following sentences to construct a sequential story of about five pages:

1. This relationship never had a chance.
2. I'm sorry, I can't stop laughing.
3. The argument almost ended in a fistfight.
4. What's wrong with my body?
5. He spent hours looking out the window.

The purpose of this exercise is to force the students to develop a causal chain of incidents, a tougher job than you might imagine in this age of anomie. But the results were better than I'd expected. I actually got a plot of sorts with an oddly familiar overtone. Two students walking to class discuss their relationship, based principally on a one-night stand. The first is earnestly in lust, but the second is far more casual about it all and says so. By the time the conversation has reached that pass, the two students are attending a lecture. Seated two rows behind them is a third student who also happens to be the second student's current lover. I won't tell who ends up staring out the window, but it was a neat bit of interweaving. Kate handed that in.

Or maybe it's just a variation on an old theme. Jennifer wrote something quite similar, but added a further twist: a fourth student back at the dormitory, staring out the window. When this student hears what's happened through an intermediary also at the lecture, she takes a lot of prescription medication accidentally on purpose.

Cynthia didn't come to class that day. Dan said she was in the infirmary. Jennifer looked thoroughly unrepentant, but about what? Hargrove and Kate said nothing unless asked, as if they had some pact between them. I took this opportunity to discuss the difference between life and art. No one contributed much to the discussion. I ended that particular class feeling as if I hadn't taught a damn thing, and I ended up in Capper's that night trying to pick up a woman who smelled vaguely like my former girlfriend. I'd had a few gin and tonics. She said she didn't go to bed with faculty. I said I was a writer and had another drink. She said writers were even worse. I don't recall how I got home, but I remember having the teaching dream again, this time with Jennifer, completely naked, lecturing while sitting on my chest. I woke up the next morning with a bad taste in my mind.

The next open assignment had them all writing about each other. Hargrove was making definite advances to Kate of all people, in a long narrative that ended in a dimly lit corridor. Dan and Cynthia were back together, but with another body that was so obviously Jennifer that I started undressing the character in my mind. They changed the names—that was about the only cover they used, which now looked like pitifully thin wrapping. I knew then that they had always been writing about the group, only I'd been too removed to see it. I walked into class, and five heads swiveled, all moving along the same groove. Hargrove was the conscience of the group, Jennifer the id, Dan and Cynthia the lovers, and Kate the organizer.

The odd thing—or one of them—was that they didn't walk around as a group. Hargrove still ate his solitary lunches in the main cafeteria while Kate pulled out a perfectly wrapped sandwich from her book bag and ate cross-legged at the edge of the dormitory quad. So where the hell was their dimly lit corridor? I gathered from two short sketches that Jennifer smoked a great deal of pot, but she never smelled of it in class. The week that Cynthia returned, she wrote a piece that finally included all five of them at a party, talking among themselves as if they had known each other all their lives. We had a discussion on how friends, strangers, and casual acquaintances address each other.

"How about strangers turning into friends?" asked Kate seriously, her notebook open.

"How about friends growing estranged from each other?" Dan contributed, looking at nobody in particular.

No nudges, no winks. Had they known each other before the start of my class, this pentagonal cabal? What about other people—family, friends? They wrote not only exhaustively about themselves, but also about no one else. It was at this point that I tried to find out about the student who dropped the class the first week—tried and failed, his name somehow erased from the record.

I have never been on the best of terms with the rest of the faculty at Hopewell, but I had to explain what was going on to someone. So I mentioned it to the program head, a large, spade-bearded poet named Tad Ferris.

"Not something I'd worry about," he told me from behind his desk, under a picture of John Berryman. "Students always write stories like that—they're young, they're inexperienced. What else have they got to write about?" He ushered me to the door with his customary bear-like grace.

Write your own obituary.

This is always my penultimate assignment, one that the students usually enjoy because it gives them a chance to write about how unappreciated they were in life. It also demands a certain amount of fantasy, which by this point I was extremely grateful to see. Kate's career as a flutist was tragically cut short when she collapsed in the middle of an ensemble performance. No immediate survivors—but she took care to mention that there were only four people in the audience. Dan and Cynthia committed suicide in a lovers' pact, jumping from the top of the mathematics building. Their bodies were discovered by Jennifer, who died from an overdose an hour later. This group obituary was really three stories that dovetailed perfectly. I pointed out how much funnier it could have been if the three accounts hadn't matched quite so neatly—humorous slippage, wit derived from contradiction. They said nothing, but Jennifer looked pityingly at me with those brown agate eyes.

Hargrove's description was the most touching, if slightly impossible because of the point of view: there he lay on the cold stone slab, crushed by a piece of fallen masonry from the eaves of the fine arts building. A minority scholarship had already been set up in his name, the product of four anonymous benefactors.

I gently pointed out that an obituary was usually not written in the first person.

Kate came to Hargrove's defense. "Couldn't most of the details have been compiled ahead of time?"

Not the fallen roof part. So we talked about verisimilitude and whether a story had to be real to induce belief in the reader. Jennifer half-recalled a phrase about the willing suspension of something or other. We ended up echoing Aristotle: better a real-sounding impossibility than an implausible possibility. We left on the margin—we will always leave on the margin—the distinction between fiction and fact. All I suggested was that they use their imaginations.

The last assignment was open: anything they cared to do.

"Now that we're all dead," commented Jennifer, "what is there left to write about?"

I smiled benignly. "I can't even begin to guess."

Why didn't I anticipate the obvious? Or is that simply a feature of hindsight? Cynthia handed in a short story about a writer who once finished a novel and then couldn't complete another. Hargrove wrote a sketch about a man who looks for love in a bar every night. Dan compiled an absorbing bildungsroman, if that's the right term for a piece of seven pages. It went from cradle to thirty-three and included background details that he had no right to know. Kate's was more along the lines of a portrait: a well-meaning but somewhat shy professor who doesn't really understand his students. But it was Jennifer's story that bothered me the most. It concerned a writing teacher who fixates on a member of his class, to the point where he starts to fantasize about her and finally calls at her apartment.

What bothered me most wasn't the innuendo but the predictive element. All the other stories described where I'd been; this one pointed where I was going. It made me deadly curious, to say the least.

So here I am at nine P.M. on Thursday, the day after the class has ended. I'm standing on the doorstep of apartment #5 at 17 Chestnut Street, and I've just rung the bell. The smudged, indecipherable nameplate doesn't resolve whether Jennifer really lives here. But someone must, whether it's Kate or Dan or Cynthia or Hargrove. And by this point I need to know, having suspended my beliefs—or disbeliefs—for entirely too long.

I ring the bell a second time and take a step back from the door, waiting for an answer.

THE LANDLORD

THE FIRST TIME I complained to my landlord Pedro about the apartment, it was regarding the lights, which tended to fade in the evenings. He said he'd send the electrician the next day, so I spent that night reading by the glow of a vespers candle borrowed from the Cathedral of the Assumption. The next afternoon around three o'clock, the man showed up and mostly fixed the situation (afterwards the lights faded in the afternoon, when it didn't matter so much). He fiddled with the fusebox, drove a screwdriver into a slot that I thought would electrocute him, and somehow managed to achieve a strobe effect in my Moroccan lamp. But he replaced what looked like a faulty piece of wiring and inserted a new fuse in the main panel. During the whole procedure, he talked hardly at all and refused a glass of aguardiente with a brief "*No gracias.*"

The odd part of the affair was the electrician himself, who I could have sworn was Pedro in a disguise with a toothbrush mustache. He had the same gaunt build, somewhat hidden in voluminous green overalls. But he'd cut and slicked back his hair, and his bony nose supported a pair of heavy horn-rimmed glasses. Besides talking with him over the telephone in my halting Spanish, I'd met Pedro only once before, so I couldn't be entirely sure. His cough, a dry substitute for speech, sounded familiar, but so what? Still, the vision bothered me for several days, chiefly when I was turning my lamp on or off. I finally dismissed the idea as absurd and went back to why I'd come to Cuernavaca, which was to finish the first draft of my interminable memoir.

Two months later, when I needed the sink fixed, I called Pedro and told him, "*Fregadero no funciona.*" My Spanish was at best an improvised affair—picture a man in half-lit darkness, rummaging in a box of nouns and verbs—but I could utter sentences. I could also usually understand the sense of what people said to me, using half-remembered cognates and some French tarnished with age. In any event, it didn't take long to get the gist of the reply: *plomero, martes.*

The plumber promised for Tuesday was definitely Pedro in a graying wig and stained undershirt. The lifts he'd put in his espadrilles to make himself taller didn't fool me, but I pretended that he was Almodovar the plumber, as he announced himself. He poked around with a mottled wrench, crouching under the pipes and muttering about leakages. From time to time, he coughed into his undershirt. Eventually, he reached into a U-shaped bend and triumphantly plucked out a hunk of gristle and hair. Gesturing about proper use of the drain sieve, with an interjection or two in a querulous old man's voice, he packed up his tools and departed. I watched from my second-story window to see when he would throw off his disguise, but he simply got into a van labeled "Plomería Almodovar" and drove off. That sign on the side of the van, I thought, was a nice touch.

This time, I wrote about the incident to my friend Petrushka, still living in Caracas after all these years. "You will be amused to hear," I typed on my old Remington, "that my landlord is a man of a thousand faces." I described how a little rouge or hair dye could alter the familiar—not beyond recognition, but more along the lines of Freud's definition of the uncanny: the expected, thrown slightly off. My letter went on for several pages, partly because I was lonely that day, but also because I was trying to work out this peculiarity in my writing. The American expatriate is always confronting these sly alterations, from the barbershop's standard clientele of old men, but reading foreign newspapers and talking of soccer matches, to the fish served in the sidewalk café, like trout but for all those extra little bones. Perhaps everything is simply a matter of accent and echo.

For that matter, Cuernavaca wasn't the first city where I'd started my memoir, this project of self-recovery. Tentatively called *Mimicking a Life*, it was intended to stretch from my apprentice days as a foreign correspondent to my career as a novelist who broadened into a man of letters over some forty years. During the course of my profession, I'd lived in Buenos Aires, Guadeloupe, Marrakesh, Caracas—all places where I'd begun sketching notes for this volume. I had plenty to write about: for example, you couldn't reside in any postwar Latin American country without getting embroiled in the Communist Party, even if you'd been a Republican back home. And in Guadeloupe, I became acquainted with the local underworld through a crime boss named Pierre le Propriétaire, just because we shared similar hours at the Café Bouchoir.

But my point, if a memoir can be said to have a thesis, was that all these events were mere window dressing to my interior life. The contents of my notebook came mostly from my imagination, not my experiences, which could just as well have progressed in a closet in Detroit if the writing were going well. I was married once, early in my career, but when I expressed these sentiments to my wife, Petrina, she wisely decamped. For most people, art is a likeness borrowed from life, but for me it was Oscar Wilde's inversion: a life that resembled art. Whenever I saw a particularly resplendent view through a window, I looked around for a mirror to catch its reflection.

The problem with the memoir was that the traits of my individuals had begun to mix and merge, from the exophthalmic gaze of my old boss at the *Herald Tribune* to the fish-eye of the groundskeeper I met on my walks through the Jardín Borda, and whose pronounced limp I in turn transferred to a middle-aged prostitute I'd known in Argentina. This wasn't a problem I had when writing fiction. I went back to my notebooks, only to find that I'd recorded nothing of these particulars, being always more preoccupied at the time with creating characters for my novels.

As for Pedro, he reminded me of someone I'd met just after the war, a shopkeeper in Rouen who presided over a jewelry store, a rather grim business since half his stock looked as if it had been plundered from refugees: matched rings, cameo lockets, silver cigarette cases, and other domestic treasure. Both men had the same matter-of-fact aspect: This is what life throws up, they seemed to say. Take it or leave it. For his part, Pedro went about his fix-it jobs as if maintaining a clock that lost a little more time each day. As his southern shrugs indicated, anything was bound to run down eventually.

My own sense of time began to run backwards, befitting a man writing his memoirs. Thirty-five years earlier my first novel, *The Impersonation*, had swum into print. The author photo displayed a bearded young man with a jaunty air, which in itself was a bit of impersonation (the beard was grown specially for the portrait, the lighthearted demeanor borrowed from a friend). In fact, the book took too long to emerge, and I'd never been entirely happy with the way it presented itself. Yet after four more novels, a book of stories, and two collections of essays, I was still facing the intolerable wrestle with words and meanings. In fact, in a way it was getting worse: what I was writing bumped up against what I'd written, with reverberations I couldn't quell.

This kind of close concentration on language made life a little

shadowy, or what I could glean of it by the view from my uphol-
stered cave. Perhaps for this reason I'd always written best in a
country where I couldn't quite understand the local patois, the
daily commerce of pleasantries and arguments. My Spanish had
always been crude, despite occasional efforts to improve it; hence,
Argentina, Venezuela, Mexico.

Now this same principle worked against me. When I called
Pedro on the telephone, we got little further than discussing another problem with the apartment. Who are you, really? I wanted
to ask, and instead found myself repeating, in my half-comical
Spanish, "*Puerta de la ropero esta rota*," "My closet door is broken." That would at least ensure a visit from the carpenter, who
came the following week.

In the meantime, I tried to get out a little more and actually
made inquiries around town. Cuernavaca had become a prosper-
ous city since the time of Malcolm Lowry, with the *barranca* no
longer a chasm but a picturesque ravine. The neighborhood where
I lived, near the Teopanzolco Pyramid, that odd pentahedron en-
closing a smaller one, had become a bustle of shops and restaurants, especially around Calle Amacuzac. One day I asked the
baker's wife, a tall, strong-armed woman who spoke some English,
what she knew about Pedro. She coughed and folded her arms
across her chest.

"He doesn't come around here," she said. "No children. I think
his wife is dead." And that was all she was able to tell me. I asked
at a few other places but got what I was beginning to recognize as
the local shrug, a hunch where the shoulders stayed in place while
the body sagged. "*No sé, no sé.*" Where did Pedro live, anyway? All
I knew was a post office box in Taxco, where I sent the monthly
rent. Since I'd gotten my apartment by answering a small advertisement in *El Mundo*, I tried to track down the listing. But when

I called the newspaper office, I was told they had no record of such a notice. I decided to wait.

The carpenter came on Tuesday in a van that looked like Almodovar the plumber's. He hoisted out a gigantic wooden toolbox full of saws, drills, and other sharp tools. At first, he looked like one of the porters at the train station, surly and stooped from decades of valises and trunks. His face was broader and flatter than I remembered, his voice rough as a rasp. He called himself Ricardo and accepted my offer of a drink, though he stuck to Sidral. Then he went at my closet door with force, unseating the hinges, brusquely pointing out the problem (the screw holes were loose), and driving in the hinges an inch higher where the wood was still good. I couldn't complain, especially since I'd yanked the door out of kilter myself, deliberately. He wore gray trousers and a baggy denim shirt, and I mentally compared the image with Pedro the plumber and Pedro the electrician. Not too similar. But when he paused to view his handiwork, he rubbed his forefinger against the base of his narrow nose. That was a trademark gesture, and I saw him for who he was.

It was all I could do to avoid clapping him on the back and letting him know. I don't know why I didn't; it was somehow part of the game. His eyes of blandest brown, the shade of the coffee cup from which I drank every morning, betrayed nothing. His cough had altered in timbre but kept the same value, like a punctuation mark. I tipped him five pesos and watched him drive away, merging with the neighborhood traffic. The late afternoon sun glinted off the rear bumper, casting a dented chrome halo.

Work on the memoir crept along during the summer. I wrote down notes, an outline, pages of false starts, another outline, but none of this helped when I sat down to type. I always seemed to be writing someone else's life, another person's intimacies. I was describing a one-armed Russian soldier named Piotr I'd met in

Marrakesh when I realized that he was lifted from my novel *One Another*. And an incident concerning three black cats and a seamstress, I realized, was the basis of a short story in Caracas from twenty years ago. All complete fiction.

I tried hard to concentrate on my own life, regularly visiting the Palacio, but the paintings there thrust me back into the world of reflections, and the haunting Diego Rivera mural began to invade my dreams. I took solitary walks along Hidalgo Street under the cooling shade of the laurel trees, but then I'd be tempted by some guava juice from a fruit vendor or hear the strains of a mariachi band, and my carefully reconstructed memories would unravel. The work went slowly, slowly. Each night before I fell asleep, I stared at the asymmetrical shadow from my bedroom window, trying to separate what I'd really experienced from what I'd merely written about. During the day I went out less and less, out of some vague fear of existential contamination.

Do you know what it's like to lose yourself this way, all familiarity slowly draining into the streets of an alien city? If this had happened in Buenos Aires or Marrakesh, I'd probably been too engrossed with my fiction to notice. Here, I felt like a character myself, maybe even the victim of a plot. People on the street occasionally nodded to me as if I knew them, or else they pretended not to have heard me. My days developed odd narrative jumps—I'd find myself seated on a park bench with no idea of how I got there, or walking with a paper bag that contained something peculiar like pumice or saltpeter. Back at my apartment, the view from my second-story oriel had become erratic: a kiosk that disappeared and reappeared, an apartment building on the corner that changed its height. Eventually, these aberrations affected my health.

In September, I came down with what the Mexicans call a chill, which at its worst is a virulent flu. The sniffles gave me a sore throat, which spread its ache throughout my body in heat waves. It finally got so bad that I was reduced to bed. "*Necesito un méd-ico*" was a sentence I'd memorized, but I called Pedro, my only real contact, to send me a doctor. I don't think I have to tell you who attended me, with his cold stethoscope and gruff bedside manner. His gray three-piece suit buttoned badly over his angular frame. Looking down at my prostrate form, he pensively brushed his finger against his nose. Instructing me to cough, he did so him-self. He told me to take two white pills, which I later identified as aspirin, and drink plenty of *agua*. Do you make more money these days as a doctor than as an electrician? I felt like asking. I was feeling too weak to see what kind of van he left in. Then, for a while, the delirium of my fever prevented me from posing any questions at all. I saw double wherever I looked, sometimes even triple.

My recovery took longer than expected. At sixty-five, I no longer possessed the resiliency of youth or even the pliability of middle age. When I finally groped my way out of bed, I was left with occasional dizzy spells, the ache of my bones transmuted into joint trouble. The only person who saw me with any fre-quency was a bartender named Pereira at a cantina on Tejada Street, since I found that a glass of mescal in the evenings eased the pain. I kept working desultorily on my memoir, but nothing held together for me. I let all my correspondence pile up on my desk, including two unanswered letters from my friend Petrushka. I neglected to pay the rent, perhaps to tease out the force that Pedro had become.

Maintaining a daily routine of reading and walking, I attempted to work as much out of fear as habit. My mind kept my body mov-ing the way an old man whips his mule. In the evenings, I dropped by the cantina. "*Mescal, poquito*," I would tell Pereira, his thin, lugubrious figure hunched over the zinc bar. Behind him stood all the refracting glasses and bottles, which I'd gaze at whenever I found the physical presence of Pereira too disquieting. A month went by, or maybe a season. The weather stays pretty much the same in Cuernavaca, each day a duplicate of the next, so it was hard to tell. The mariachi bands played all the time, and nothing ever seemed to end. This life offered repetition without closure.

One afternoon as I was painfully climbing the rickety stairs to my apartment, I felt a sudden numbness along my left side. I cried out—no sound came. I grabbed for the railing, but my hand closed on a fistful of icy air. The floor of the stairwell had somehow landed on my chest. I looked upwards, craning my neck, but the available light fled through the window on the landing.

Somehow I managed to reach my apartment. Petrushka appeared at my door. She had come to visit me, but when I brought her into my study, she turned to one side and I saw the profile of Pedro, his nose casting a pointed shadow on the closet door. I ran into the streets, but the first passerby I accosted was dressed in Pedro's shapeless overalls, his dull sienna eyes gazing right through me. I fled in the opposite direction. Pedro the policeman blew his whistle, the shrill tone piercing my skull. Roused by the sound, Pedro the baker, Pedro the tailor, and Pedro the café waiter chased after me. They were joined by Pedro the mechanic and Pedro the garage owner. They grew into an army of Pedros, closing in on me from every block.

I ran until my legs betrayed me. They caught up to me at the Chapel of the Third Order, where they bound me and hoisted my body onto their shoulders. I couldn't breathe, couldn't think. The next I knew, I was lying in a long dark room. My limbs were petrified, cold as the veined marble effigies I'd once seen in St. Peter's church. Unable to move, I waited there an hour, a day, who knows?

Finally the door creaked open, and a black-robed and hooded

figure glided in. I hoped for a rosary, for the comforting symbol of the silver crucifix dangling from the front, but I couldn't turn my head that way, and the silhouette on the wall looked far older than Calvary. Soon he was hovering over me. Even before he pushed back the hood slightly to rub a bony forefinger against his missing nose, I knew who it was. The cough, when it arrived, was eternal.

Pedro, coming to collect.